Stell-Ore Justice

Stell-Ore War, Volume 2

J.I. O'Neal

Published by Bolidium Press, 2020.

STELL-ORE JUSTICE

First edition. June 1, 2020.

Copyright © 2020 J.I. O'Neal.

ISBN: 978-1393868057

Written by J.I. O'Neal.

Also by J.I. O'Neal

Riverdale PD Series
Impact: A Riverdale PD Series Prequel
Indiscriminate: 5th Anniversary Revised Edition
Time of Death

Stell-Ore War
The Crew of Cartage 15
Stell-Ore Justice

A note about pronunciation:

Darius Alazar = duh-RYE-us uh-LA-zahr
Bolidium = Bo-LID-EE-um
Meris Brand = MARE-us BRAND
Fydach Cale = FIDD-ick CALE
Zac Colphin = ZACK COLE-fin
Egalia/-n = ee-GAL-ee-uh/-un
Berent Gaehts = BARE-unt GETS
Myranda Gaehts = Mer-RAN-da GETS
Leo Hull = Lee-o HUHL
Edzard Kier = ED-zerd KEER
Wyll Meiryg = WILL MY-rig
Minos/-ian = MINE-os/MY-no-zhun
Nevzaris = NEV-zurr-iss
Pentra/Pentarian = PEN-truh/PEN-tair-ee-un
Rieka/-n = RYE-kuh/ken
Sendrassa/-n = sen-DRASS-uh/-un
Sindria/-n = SEND-ree-uh/un
Thalassa = thuh-LASS-uh
Tudorya/-n = too-DOR-ee-uh/-un

CHAPTER 1 – MYRANDA

"Internal bleeding, bruised ribs, broken nose, broken fingers on both hands, contusions and lacerations virtually everywhere...it's a miracle he survived the journey here."

Myranda Gaehts gave the doctor a grateful smile. "Thank you for saving his life. I cannot tell you how important he is to me."

Doctor Loken, a middle-aged man with pale blonde hair and light blue eyes typical of all Sindrians, repaid her smile with a nod. "Your husband is very lucky to have had you looking out for him, Mrs. Stellerson."

She tried not to cringe at the false name she had given to protect herself and Darius Alazar from her real husband, Berent Gaehts. She knew Berent would be checking all the hospitals on Sindria for them and couldn't risk being found while Alazar was so vulnerable. "Can I see him now?"

The doctor nodded once more. He's not likely to be very coherent yet, but he's stable enough for a short visit. If you'll follow me."

She followed Loken down the hall to the recovery ward. This hospital was surprisingly similar to the one she worked in back in Nordfylke. Maybe all hospitals on this planet were the same? The doctor showed her in to Alazar's room, saying he'd come back in fifteen minutes when visitation ended and giving her strict instructions not to overtire her husband. She promised she'd behave and waited until he had gone before turning her attention to her patient.

Alazar was asleep. His usually handsome face- as far as Sindrians went, anyway- was swollen and stitched in various places. The heart monitor emitted a strong, steady rhythm and his breathing was even and slow. She went to the niche in the footboard of the bed and removed his chart, the touchpad's screen waking up at her touch. Alazar's medical record displayed on the screen and she flipped through its pages, looking for any issues she'd need to monitor him for over the coming days. Other than the usual risk of post-operative infection, he appeared to be in no immediate danger.

"Meris?"

She looked up to see him squinting at her. She put the chart back into its niche and came closer to him, brushing a lock of her long red-streaked black hair away from her face. "No, Alazar, it's Myranda. Meris is with the others waiting for us. How do you feel?"

He grunted and licked his busted lips. "Like I barely survived being beaten to death."

His voice was hoarse. She picked up a cup of water from the bedside table and helped him take a sip. He swallowed thickly. "Thank you."

Relentlessly polite, our Alazar. "You bet."

She eyed him a little more closely. He looked so frail, nothing like the powerful magnate he was just a few days ago as owner of Stell-Ore Mining Company, the Newverse's largest supplier of Bolidium- the versatile and lucrative ore used for pretty much everything. He had always seemed untouchable and yet somehow so compassionate. In the days she'd gotten to know him, she realized that persona was genuine. He was a caring, noble man.

He was also the man her husband was framing for mass murder.

"I'm going to have to get you out of here soon. Do you think you'll be up for it?"

He nodded slowly. "I know you'll take care of me." He tried to smile but it ended up a wince. He let out a slow, controlled breath before asking, "How soon?"

Myranda glanced out the window. Evening was fast approaching. "After the four o'clock rounds but before sunrise." She frowned sympathetically. "I'd give you more time if I could..."

"I'll be fine."

She gave a curt nod. "You have to be, or Berent wins." Her hands balled into fists. "And I can't let that happen."

Out of the corner of her eye, she saw Doctor Loken through the sidelight of the door. He rapped his knuckles on the glass before entering the room. She forced her hands and expression to relax and smiled at him, giving Alazar's forearm a subtle warning squeeze.

"Fifteen minutes already?"

"I'm afraid so, Mrs. Stellerson. Your husband needs to rest now."

She turned back to Alazar and gave him the warmest smile she could fake. "You heard the doctor, honey. Get some rest now; I'll be back in the morning."

He barely batted an eye. "I'll look forward to it, my love."

She bent as if to kiss him but made a show of stopping herself at the sight of his many wounds. "Oh, um..." she said, straightening back up and kissing her fingertips and pressing them to his left temple, one of the few uninjured spots on his face.

"Good night, love," she told him. The loving look he gave her was so convincing she felt her heart skip a beat. *Should've been an actor.*

He placed his battered hand over hers. "Be safe."

She smiled again, though she was far from happy to leave him unguarded, and turned to face the doctor. The look of suspicion on his face was quickly concealed by a warm smile. She forced her features to remain neutral, not conveying the fear that made her heart now thud. "Good night, Doctor."

"Good night."

His voice was steady and expression didn't falter, but there was an undercurrent that told her she hadn't imagined him putting it together that the badly beaten Sindrian man and the Tudoryan woman before him may not be who they said they were. But he stepped aside for her and she gave Alazar one last parting glance, warning him to watch out for the seemingly good-natured caregiver, before leaving the room.

Out in the hallway, she kept her pace even and confident as she headed for the exit. If Loken knew who they were, Alazar was in danger, and not just from her husband. Every law enforcement agency on this colony-planet were looking for him. They may need to step up their timetable by several hours.

She pulled her vid-phone out of her pocket and sent a buzz to her brother, Wyll.

Possibly sussed. Ready the fireworks. -M

CHAPTER 2 – MERIS

"You're going to stay well clear, right?"

Wyll sighed. "Yes."

She was aggravating him with all her worrying. It didn't matter; they could not afford any mistakes. "Leo and I will be too far away to help you if you blow yourselves up." She caught herself chewing on her lower lip and pressed her mouth into a tight line to stop.

"Miss Brand –"

"Meris."

Wyll's jaw clenched and unclenched. "Meris. We've been over this with a fine-toothed comb; everything will be all right." The young Tudoryan soldier was better than most of his countrymen at keeping his expression neutral, but his irritation was clear in the way he tugged at the hem of the blue and white diamond-patterned shirt Leo had lent him.

"What if it isn't?" She rubbed her thumb and forefinger on the dog tags hanging around her neck over the plain long-sleeved blue shirt Leo had given her. *Ellias Martijn Gammett, Cartage Crew Chief, O positive, Christian.* Four lines of bare facts on two metal ovals on a chain, they were her last connection to the man she had planned to marry, one of the many victims of Berent Gaehts' deranged ambition.

This time, the look Wyll gave her was more sympathetic. She still wasn't used to seeing him out of his Stell-Ore Security uniform, especially not masked by the helmet's blank face shield, and was only beginning to understand the shifts in his expression. "Don't worry," he told her, "Zac and I have got this down cold. Just concentrate on your part and the rest will fall into place. Okay?"

She nodded, then went back to filling the metal canister on the workbench in front of her with gunpowder. It had been almost twenty-four hours since she and the others had escaped the Stell-Ore compound – barely – with Alazar, but it already felt like a lifetime ago. In a way, it was.

Leo knocked on the workshop door before he and Zac entered. The former, a slender Sendrassan man, seemed to have recovered from his near-death experience at Stell-Ore and the latter, a taller Egalian, had one hand lightly touching the spot on his side where he had been clipped by a HEL-gun. They carried a pair of backpacks in and placed them on the workbench.

"You don't have to knock, Leo; you own the place."

His eyes shifted toward Wyll, who was busy taking apart another set of bullets. "I didn't want to interrupt."

"It's fine," she assured him. "We were just going over the plan."

Leo rubbed his hand across his narrow chin. "Do you think I should shave before we go? I don't want to look..." He shrugged vaguely.

"Like you fit in?" Wyll looked at him over his shoulder. "Medics and doctors always look like crap. We may be light-years away from Earth, but our medical technology isn't too radically different. It still requires actual human beings taking care of other human beings, and that means long hours."

"Are you saying your sister always looks like crap?" Zac asked.

Surprisingly, Wyll grinned. "Only most of the time."

His vid-phone emitted a chime. He got it out of his pocket and frowned at the screen. "Speaking of..." He read silently a moment, then set the phone down with a muttered curse.

"What is it?" She and Zac asked simultaneously.

"Buzz from Myranda. She thinks she and Alazar may have been discovered. We need to get this ready ASAP." He gathered up the gunpowder he'd taken from the bullets and dumped it into the canister she held. "Let's go."

Meris' heart began to race. "It's too early, there'll be too many people." Regardless, she put the lid on the canister and tucked it under her arm.

Zac looped one backpack over his shoulder and handed the other to Leo. He grabbed his tablet and vid-phone, shoving them both into pockets and said, "She's right, Wyll, the area will be full."

Leo added, "Someone could get hurt."

Wyll shrugged, but Meris detected a hint of worry in his jade eyes. "I'll find somewhere there's nobody around. I'm not going to let anyone get hurt, but if they do, at least they'll be in the best place."

CHAPTER 3 – MERIS

T*he hospital is too busy. This is a stupid idea, a big mistake. It's already too late and Berent is already here looking for us. He's gonna-*

"You still with us?" Zac gave her a lopsided grin when she looked up, startled out of her thoughts.

Her brow crinkled in a worried frown. "Where do you think he is right now?" Her forehead was going to become permanently furrowed from all the stress of this past week. The knot in her stomach felt twice as big today as it did yesterday.

Zac took a long moment before answering, letting his gaze wander over the interior of the Personnel Transporter Vehicle Wyll was flying them in to get to their rendezvous point. "He skipped out before we did, so he probably went to ground. If he knows we survived, which we don't know for sure he does, then there's about a fifty-fifty chance he's looking to silence us before we get to the Nexus Hub."

Leo frowned. "Why only fifty?"

"If it were the other way around," Zac asked them, "what would your main concern be right now?"

Meris shrugged. "Making sure no one knows the truth."

He nodded. "The way I see it, there are exactly two ways to do that. And if he doesn't want to risk exposure by killing us all, his only other option is to discredit us."

"So, you're saying he's either looking for us or he's heading to a Nexus Hub, too," Meris said.

"Bingo."

Leo let out a slow breath. "I never thought of that possibility."

She had to swallow before she could speak again. Her mouth was still dry. "That's... How do we stop him?"

Zac shook his head, scoffing. "The only thing we can do is beat him to the punch. Literally or figuratively."

"We're going in now." Wyll's voice sounded loud after their hushed conversation. "Everyone ready?"

The three exchanged looks. "As we'll ever be," Zac answered for them.

Meris slammed through the double doors into the hospital lobby. "Somebody help!"

She ran to the nurses' station, where a group of four nurses and three doctors were gathered. "Please," she begged, "there's been an explosion!"

Without hesitation, they all sprang into action. One doctor placed a hand on her shoulder and examined her face. "Where? What happened? Are you injured?"

"In the woods behind the park." She swallowed and gulped in another breath. "I don't know how far- maybe a quarter of a mile? I was in the park, there was this loud boom. I'm all right. I'm fine."

She swayed a bit and he held her up. She gripped his lab coat as tight as she could in her fists. "All I could see was smoke.

I think there were other people closer- you have to help them. Please help them!"

"All right, miss, stay here."

He rushed to join the other personnel as they exited the lobby. She overheard one of the nurses say, "There! I see the smoke!" And one of the doctors told the one she had spoken to, "Call the fire units, I'll get the ambulances dispatched."

She made a point to stay looking miserable and scared until they were out of sight. Even though, technically, everything she said was true, it still galled her to play this role. *Forgive me this deception, Lord. Both of them.*

She noted the two other people in the lobby. An elder man and a young woman, both Sindrian, had abandoned their seats and now stood at the entry. They kept looking back and forth between her and out the windows with wide eyes.

"I need... I need a drink. There's a dispenser around here somewhere, right?" She turned and wandered down the hallway, toward the recovery wing. After she made the turn down the first intersecting hallway, she sent a buzz to Wyll:

Seven on their way to you. Getting to M and A now.

Myranda glanced around the door frame and let out a relieved sigh when she saw Meris. "Where'd you get all that?"

Meris held up the keycard she'd slipped off the doctor's lab coat and now had affixed to a lab coat of her own. "I found the supply room and borrowed a few things."

Myranda grinned at her. "Get in here. I snuck back in after the doctor left, but he could come back any minute."

Meris followed her into Alazar's room. He lay in the bed, nearly every bit of his face swollen and discolored and patched with bandages and splints. The sight of him sent a sharp jolt through her stomach, but he smiled at her as well as he could.

"Hello there, Doctor. Can I go home now?"

"Anywhere but, I'm afraid." She sent a buzz to Leo, letting him know they were in place. "We've got about five minutes, maximum," she told Myranda.

Myranda nodded and began shutting off Alazar's machines. Meris took a set of rolled-up scrubs out of her pocket and sat them on the bed. "I figured they threw out your clothes."

"Thank you." He sat up as carefully as he could, grunting with pain and effort.

Feeling the time crunch, Meris pulled the blankets back for him, then ducked to help him put an arm around her shoulders. He hissed in a sharp breath as she stood him up, and Myranda eyed him with concern as she removed the monitor leads from his chest and brought the IV stand to the other side of the bed.

"Sorry," Meris told him. "You okay?"

He winced but nodded. "I'll be fine," he said, panting.

Myranda picked up a touchpad fitted into a niche in the footboard. "Meris, let me see that keycard."

Meris handed it over, then helped Alazar brace himself against the chair next to the bed. "Here," she said, taking out the scrub pants and knelt to help him step into them. She had to ignore the rush of pink that flushed both of their faces as it became apparent he was naked beneath the hospital gown and she pulled the pants up as quickly as possible. They were still blushing as she helped him take the gown off and put on the scrubs shirt.

His entire torso was a mass of bruises and cuts. But what caught her attention the most was the surgical incision site. About two inches long, the red gash made a vertical line to the right and slightly above his navel. It had been sealed with surgical glue, but still looked like it would leave a scar. Actually, he would probably end up with multiple scars.

The hardest part of the process proved to be getting his arms into the sleeves. Raising his arms elicited pain from the incision and the broken fingers on each hand kept catching painfully on the material. But after a tense few moments, she finally had him dressed. The sound of a small craft approaching told her their time was up and they weren't in place yet. "That's Leo," she informed the other two.

Myranda had gathered an armload of medical supplies, using the keycard to unlock the cabinet on the wall. "Ehm," she said, looking around. She finally laid the bottles, bandages and extra IV bags on the bed and bundled them up in Alazar's hospital gown. "Okay, I'm ready."

Myranda led the way, peeking out into the hallway for a moment first. "It's clear," she said. "Come on."

Meris and Alazar followed her into the hall, every step a challenge for the tall Sindrian man. He made no complaints, however, and the trio soon made it to the end of the corridor. He was panting and pale but was keeping up. So far.

"Wait here a second." Myranda disappeared into the intersecting corridor, then came back a few seconds later. "All clear. Let's get out of here."

Meris spied an empty hover-capable wheelchair sitting idle in the corner. "Hold on," she told Myranda.

She guided Alazar toward the wheelchair and helped him sit. With her much smaller stature, she would have tired out too quickly before they made it to the roof. There was no way he would have been able to bear his own weight and she was glad she now didn't have to support him the whole way.

Alazar groaned a little, but sank back into the hoverchair in evident relief. She pushed the power switch and it juddered forward and lifted a few inches off the floor at her command. Steering him as fast as she could without drawing any unwanted attention, they passed several rooms before nearing the lobby. Meris didn't look to see if the man and woman from before were still around, focusing more on looking like a doctor transporting a patient, and they hurried toward a bank of elevators behind the nurses' station.

Myranda pressed the 'UP' button and the door slid open a moment later. They ducked inside and she had to wave the keycard in front of the reader on the control panel in order to press the button for the roof. Alazar placed a hand to his stomach as the elevator lurched upward.

"You all worked this out pretty well." He sounded impressed.

Myranda smirked. "Glad you think so."

"We're sort of making it up as we go, actually," Meris said, looking down at him. "We were so fixated on working out the explosion, we sort of glossed over a few of the finer points of your... extraction."

His eyebrows raised. "Well done, then."

She and Myranda chuckled, feeling some of the tension ease off. The elevator door slid open to reveal a short hallway that ended in a metal door. A keycard reader blinked red next to it. Myranda rushed forward and waved the card.

Nothing happened.

She looked at them. "Ehm, let's try that again." She waved the card again, quicker this time. Still the light blinked red at them. She growled in frustration and waved it again.

"Maybe slower?"

Myranda glanced at her irritably, but then tried it again much more slowly. A small click preceded the light turning green. They all breathed a sigh of relief.

She threw open the door and the last rays of golden evening sunlight bouncing off the light-colored roof momentarily dazzled their eyes. The quiet roar of the small transporter's thrusters reverberated off the various structures dotting the roof and Meris could feel its vibrations in her chest. Leo waved to them from the pilot's seat impatiently.

The sirens of the rescue vehicles responding to the staged explosion rang out in a chorus from the opposite side of the building below. Meris helped Myranda get Alazar out of the hoverchair and onto the transporter before climbing in themselves. They had no room for the hoverchair, so they had to leave it behind in the middle of the landing pad.

Once they were in safely, Leo took off, staying at the height of the roofline until they were well away from the hospital. He took them across an open meadow and then dropped low as they approached a mag-lev track. Switching over to mag-lev mode, the transporter slowed and began to follow the track of its own accord. Leo swiveled the pilot's chair to face the three of them.

"Glad to see you in one piece, Mr. Alazar," Leo told his boss, who now lay in the open floor space between rows of seats. "More or less."

"You, too, Leo. Where are Zac and Wyll?"

"On their way to the next rendezvous point."

Myranda furrowed her brow. "Are they okay?"

"Right as rain," Leo nodded. "Whatever that means. I got a buzz from Zac right before I picked you guys up saying they were safely in place and would check in again at midnight and six a.m."

"We aren't meeting up with them tonight, then?" Alazar asked.

"No sir, not until tomorrow, I'm afraid. We need to give you time to rest, to make sure you're fit enough to go on camera first."

Myranda, seated next to Meris in the row behind him, nudged Alazar with her foot before he could protest. "Doctor's orders, so don't argue."

"Yes, ma'am," he said with a tinge of amusement in his voice.

He winked at Meris, his eyes sparkling with humor, despite the heavy bruising around them. Her stomach clenched up as he looked at her, just as it had when he had offered his condolences on the loss of her fiancé. Even knowing now that he had nothing to do with Ellias' death, it was hard for her to shake that initial distrust and contempt that had fueled her to infiltrate Stell-Ore and accuse him publicly. And just as hard to shake her guilt for inciting the riot that had allowed Berent to overthrow Alazar – and beat him nearly to death. She hadn't yet had time to reconcile the conflicting emotions this man evoked, but now that they were on the same side, she was attempting to see him as her ally and let go of the rest.

She gave him a small smile in return before turning her attention to the Sindrian countryside through which they now traveled. Rolling green meadows stretched in all directions, dotted with tiny blue flowers called Swans-bonnets. She never understood the name, the five-petaled blooms resembled neither swans nor a bonnet. Maybe the name was a carry-over from Earth, from as far back in antiquity as bonnets themselves were.

As a child, she had often made crowns of the lovely blossoms, wearing them and proclaiming herself queen of the swans. That was many, many years ago, but she always somehow felt peaceful and safe when she saw them growing. Tonight, however, that feeling eluded her. Dread for what lay ahead of them seeped through every part of her being until it felt like Berent was right behind them or waiting somewhere up the track for them.

She closed her eyes, conjuring images of Ellias in the sunlight, when he looked most alive and vibrant and at peace with the world. In her mind's eye, he smiled and told her everything would be all right. She leaned her head against the back of her seat, a tear trailing down her face in the uncertain twilight.

CHAPTER 4 – MERIS

When she woke, the sky was full dark. The pale rosy glow of the moon softly brushed over the landscape. It's light cast shadows that made the interior of the transporter seem foreign.

"Sorry."

Alazar's voice was a warm whisper in the shadows. She realized then that it had been his leg brushing against hers that had woken her. "It's okay." She glanced at the others, who were still sleeping. "Why aren't you asleep? Do you need anything?"

"I don't sleep much, generally speaking." He shifted a bit with a grunt of effort, scooting further from where Myranda was dozing and closer to Meris. "Can I ask you something, Miss Brand?"

She nodded, then realized he probably couldn't see her well enough to know that. "Of course."

"Are you positive you're willing to accept the fallout of what we're about to do?"

Her heart began to pound at the ominous tone in his voice. "I am." She cleared her throat quietly to rid her voice of the quaver that betrayed her. "I know it will be difficult and ugly, but I can't let Berent get away with this. I can't let Ellias' memory be tainted or his and all the others' deaths not be avenged."

"So, it's vengeance you want." There was a hint of disappointment in his words.

"No!" She spoke louder than she had intended to and waited a moment for Myranda to settle back into the sleep she had disturbed before continuing. "I want Berent to be brought to justice for what he's done. I want to see him in the Council's cage."

He didn't respond right away and soon she thought he must have drifted off. But then he reached up and placed his bandaged hand over hers. She was so surprised by the sudden contact that she nearly jerked her hand away. At the last moment, she stopped herself in case the motion would cause him pain.

"I admire your... passion for this crusade and your devotion to your fiancé. But please, hear me when I say I don't think you realize what's in store for us."

"And what is that?"

"A firestorm. This scandal will burn more than Berent and his supporters. It will burn me and anyone who stands with me." He removed his hand. "I don't want to see you or anyone else get hurt."

"You're not responsible for me. I started down this road with eyes wide open. I intend to see it through. I can't speak for anyone else, but that's where I stand."

He let out a slow breath. "The curse of Sindrian stick-to-itness." She detected a smile in his voice at odds with his words.

"You say that like you aren't Sindrian, too."

"Technically, I'm not."

"Oh." She wrinkled her brow. "Really?"

"My family was Earth-born. My mother – and my father, presumably – was Norwegian. My stepfather was Greek. I was born on board a starship to Minos – not the original, obviously, but one of the second generation – and was named for his father. Technically, I'm Norwegian, but was raised on Sindria. You never wondered why my name doesn't sound very Sindrian?"

"You're a starchild," she said, feeling a touch of wonder at the very idea.

He made a soft scoffing sound. "An overly romantic name, if you ask me. I don't even remember the ship, only here."

"Why here and not Minos?"

"I never knew for certain, but something happened to the ship and we had to change course. My stepfather died when I was very young, and my mother didn't like talking about that time, so I never knew details."

A loud chime interrupted before she could respond. Myranda woke up and got her vid-phone out of her pocket. Yawning behind the back of her hand, she read the buzz she'd received. She made a negative sound low in her throat.

"What is it?" Leo's voice was distorted by the yawn he spoke around.

"Wyll says to turn on the newsfeed."

Leo turned the lights up a bit inside the transporter's cabin and Meris heard Alazar groan as he covered his eyes against the dim light. Myranda pulled out her tablet and tapped the screen. The display was soon filled with the local newsfeed. Another tap and the video projected into the air above the tablet.

"*...footage shows the scale of the carnage allegedly perpetrated by Darius Colden Alazar against his own employees for protesting his authorization of the use of the extreme – and, as it turns out – unnecessary sanitation protocol, which resulted in the deaths of the entire crew of Cartage 15. We're receiving word that the riots started once it was learned that the crew members were not, in fact, infected by an off-world pathogen and that their deaths, in essence, was murder – and murder ordered by Alazar himself. We warn you, the footage you are about to see is graphic.*"

"What!?" Meris lurched forward to get a closer look, as did Leo.

Alazar simply lay there with his eyes covered.

The view of the female newscaster's face had been replaced by security footage of the firefight in the courtyard between the Stell-Ore headquarters and the Security Compound. The video was only a few seconds long. Flashes of gunfire, smoke, and debris from explosions, and the broken and bleeding bodies of miners and security officers filled their view.

Leo groaned. "Oh, this is bad."

The footage ended and the newscaster was once more on screen. "*More casualties were discovered inside the Security Compound. We're also receiving unconfirmed reports that Darius Alazar had been admitted to Hagenborg hospital under an assumed name and was subsequently smuggled out by his supporters once his real identity had been discovered by his doctor. No word has yet been received concerning the whereabouts of Lieutenant Wyll Meiryg, Officer Zac Colphin, Tech Officer Leo Hull or any other supporters of Alazar's who seem to have survived the battle.*" Wyll's, Zac's, Leo's and Alazar's ID photos were displayed on the screen.

"*Citizens are urged to notify their local police units if any of these men are seen. Also believed to be with them is Meris Brand, who is reported to have stormed the Stell-Ore headquarters in order to reveal Alazar's involvement in the criminal deaths of the cartage crew but was kidnapped by Alazar and his supporters. At this time, it is not known if Miss Brand is still living, so we urge everyone watching: do not approach or engage any of these men if seen, as this may endanger Miss Brand's life. Please notify the nearest Law Enforcement unit and let them handle the situation.*"

Myranda switched off the feed with a look of disgust. Meris looked at Leo. "Zac was right."

"Yeah." He turned to look out the window, and Meris got the impression he was savoring the view in case they were about to spend the rest of their lives in prison. Or worse.

Alazar moved his hand and Meris could see the trail of tears wandering off into his hair. "Leo, stop the vehicle."

He turned back to them abruptly. "What? But we're in the middle of nowhere."

"Stop the transporter, Mr. Hull." Alazar didn't raise his voice; he didn't need to; he was speaking as Leo's boss and the head of the most important company in the Newverse.

Leo swiveled his chair around and switched to engines, lifting the transporter up off the mag-lev track and flying it over into the grass. He landed a few hundred feet from the track and killed the engines. Swiveling his chair back around, he turned to Alazar. "Now what?"

Alazar looked up at Myranda. "Help me up."

Her expression showed how much she wanted to protest, but she set her jaw and knelt to lift him into a sitting position.

Meris then helped get him into the middle seat next to her. His breathing was labored. "Thank you." He sat there a moment with his hand on his stomach, wincing against what had to be excruciating pain.

When he looked up at them, his eyes were so very tired. "I should have known he would do this. I should have planned for it, but I didn't. And I'm sorry. Because now, all of your lives are in danger."

He looked each of them in the eye. "It's too late now to cut and run, though I wish you all could. But there is no reason for all of you to go down in flames with me."

Meris looked at the others, then at Alazar. "What exactly are you saying?"

"I'm saying go to ground. Let me confront Berent alone. I'll answer his accusations with mine on my own-"

"No. There is no way in the worlds I saved your life and risked my own just so you could martyr yourself." Myranda was deadly serious, her jade eyes glinting with hard anger.

"She's right, Mr. Alazar. We've come too far together to let you go it alone now."

Alazar nodded slowly. "Meris?"

"You know where I stand."

A smile tugged at his busted lips. "You've all lost your minds... Thank you for this." He placed his other hand across his abdomen, too, and stifled a groan. "Now, how do we want to go about proving our innocence?"

CHAPTER 5 – MYRANDA

Myranda's fists clenched as tight as they possibly could, and her jaw ached from clenching her teeth. She could never forgive Berent for everything he had done already, and now this...stunt of his was the proverbial final nail in the coffin. At least he didn't seem to know that she had sided with Alazar. Not yet, anyway. Maybe there was a way they could use that.

Everything was supposed to be so simple: get Alazar out of the Security Compound and away from Berent's men, take him to the hospital in New Friesland and then take him and Meris' vid-phone footage of the murders to the New Friesland Nexus Hub and broadcast the atrocity and Berent's role in it to the seven colony-planets. Then, they would wait for Berent to be flushed out into the open by police units, arrested and put away for good.

Now, everything was unraveling before their eyes. First, they'd had to flee New Friesland altogether and come here to Hagenborg to escape Hauher and Berent's soldiers, which cost them time, which made it so that Berent could get his twisted version of the story to the press before they could get the truth out. Now, they didn't know where to go or who they could trust. Everything was falling apart. And there wasn't a thing she could do about it.

She was clenching her jaw again. Forcing herself to open her mouth wide and work her lower jaw back and forth, she slowed her breathing and attempted to calm down. It was then that she realized she was pacing in the calf-high grass at the side of the mag-lev track.

Meris reached out and touched her arm the next time she passed by. "Hey, we'll figure something out."

She stopped and faced her. "What makes you so certain?"

Meris blinked. "Because the truth will always win out."

She snorted. "I never pegged Sindrians as being so naive."

"I'm not naive." Was that a flare of anger in the younger woman's eyes? "I have faith. Berent won't win."

This time, Myranda laughed out loud, a bitter, tired chuckle. "Oh, honey, you don't know him half as well as you think you do, if you believe that." She looked around at the others: Alazar, now seated wearily in the open doorway of the transporter, Leo hovering next to him. "Berent Gaehts always gets exactly what he wants. He may have to manipulate, coerce, or wear you down into submission, but, in the end, he's gotten what he was after. He doesn't give up until he has. Don't ever forget that."

"Then you have to tell us how to handle him." Alazar fixed her with his calm, unwavering gaze. Only the dark circles under his eyes and the sheen of sweat on his skin betrayed the pain he must be in.

Curse him and his relentless self-control! She wanted to scream. Or punch something. Or both.

"I can't imagine you spent your whole marriage caving in to this man," he continued, his hands resting lightly over the incision site. "You are far too independent and capable. You must know ways to manage him, subtly."

She crossed her arms and threw him a dark look. "Now you're starting to sound like him. Manipulative compliments are his forte." She took a breath and let it out slowly, waving her hand to dismiss the protest on his lips. "But, as it turns out, you're right. I did learn to maneuver around him, once I found out what he was really like."

Alazar tilted his head wearily toward her. "So, what do we do now?"

"I need to think." Her fingers traced slow circles on her temples. "I never thought him capable of any of this, it- it doesn't make any sense. Something had to have happened. I mean, he isn't a complete psychopath; Ellias was his best friend, he would never have hurt him or his crew unless something had gone horribly wrong." She turned to Meris. "Did Ellias ever say anything to you?"

Meris, less adept at stifling her physical expressions of emotion than Alazar, seemed to flinch at the sound of her late fiancé's name. Myranda felt a bit of a monster for making her think about him so directly, but time was of the essence. Slowly, Meris shook her head. "No, nothing that would cause this."

Alazar suddenly swore under his breath. Myranda and the others turned to him. He stared at the ground. "This really is my fault."

Meris beat her to asking. "What are you talking about?" Myranda could hear how carefully she spoke. She, like Myranda, must be trying hard not to jump to any conclusions.

Alazar put a hand to his forehead. "I don't know how he found out..."

Sweat was beaded on his brow. Myranda went over to him. His face was drained of color, leaving a sickly pallor behind. "Alazar? How are you feeling right now?"

Leo took a step closer. "Wait a minute, Myranda, let him keep talking."

She touched his forehead. It was clammy and hot. The pulse in his throat was rapid but weak. "Leo, you and Meris get back in the transporter. We need to get out of here."

Alazar grabbed her wrist in a crushing grip. "No, wait. I have to tell her," he panted. Now that his hand was no longer covering the wound, she could see bloody fluid had wicked its way through the scrub top.

"You will. But right now, you need medical attention." She looked up at Leo. "We need to get out of here now."

"Oh, no." Leo rushed to the door on the other side of the transporter and climbed in. Meris followed him.

Alazar's eyes suddenly rolled back and his grip on her wrist slackened. She made a grab for him before he tumbled out of the transporter. "Meris! Give me a hand here, please."

The Sindrian woman helped Myranda pull Alazar back into the transporter, propping him up slightly on her lap as Myranda lifted his shirt. The incision from his surgery had about a two-centimeter abscess in the middle that had begun to seep. The skin surrounding it was flushed and hot, and his pulse was racing.

She had taken what she could from the hospital room's cabinet, but she couldn't treat him effectively here. He needed a real bed inside a building where he could rest. His IV bag needed changed now, too. "We need to get to wherever we're going right now," she told Leo as she removed the gel seal and cleaned the wound.

Leo closed the transporter door behind her and jumped into the pilot seat. The vehicle started up and shot into the air, jostling the passengers. Alazar groaned and his eyes opened for a moment before sliding shut again.

Meris wiped sweat from his brow. "What's wrong with him?"

"Infection. He's going septic." She growled under her breath. "I should have given him prophylactics as soon as we left the hospital. It was so stupid not to."

Meris' eyes went wide. "Can you fix it?"

A dozen different replies flitted through her mind, none of them positive. She met Meris' gaze and held it a long moment, weighing how best to answer her. In the end, she said nothing.

CHAPTER 6 – WYLL

Wyll's vid-phone vibrated, making a loud sound on the stainless-steel countertop. He snatched it up, noticing that the buzz was from Meris instead of his sister. Puzzled, he opened it and read.

Saw newsfeed. Trying to plan next move, but Alazar took a bad turn. Septic. Myranda doing her best with what we... borrowed from the hospital.

Septic. The word sent a shockwave of worry through him. If Alazar didn't pull through... He opened a reply box, but Zac came up alongside before he could type anything.

"What did they say?" Zac's voice was hollow and raspy. Neither of them had gotten much sleep since they staged the explosion. Especially not since they arrived at Jenna's apartment. The reminders of their fallen comrade and proximity to Stell-Ore had left them feeling emotionally raw and hyper-vigilant, despite the fact they'd convinced themselves no one would look for them so close to danger.

Wyll set the phone down and rubbed his forehead. "Alazar's gone septic."

Zac paled. "He'll live, though, right? Myranda, she's gonna-"

"I don't know." He hadn't meant to growl at him, but why did everyone always assume he had all the answers?

"Okay...Okay..."

Zac sat down at the metal counter. Perched on the tall, swiveling stool next to Wyll's, he began drumming his fingers on the countertop. It was grating on Wyll's already strained nerves, but he knew better than to interrupt the Egalian man when he was strategizing.

"I've been thinking about backup plans ever since we saw how bad Alazar's injuries were," Zac said, his fingers going still. "We still have Myranda's statement and Meris' vid-phone footage-"

"Which only proves that I killed Ellias Gammett." *The crack of the airbolt and the crimson spray of the Sindrian man's blood across the snowy ground-* Wyll closed his eyes against the memory. "It proves I turned Cartage 15's own equipment against them, causing the entire crew to die under half a ton of Bolidium."

Zac turned a sympathetic look on him. "Hauher lied to you. He and Berent used you. It's not your fault."

Wyll couldn't hold back the bitter laugh that escaped him. "Do you honestly think that makes it any better?"

Zac looked away. "No. I don't suppose it does, does it?"

"That doesn't matter right now. What matters is can we avoid the Chamber if Alazar dies?"

Zac's fingers started drumming again. After a long moment, they slowed to a stop. "There's only one way I think we can."

Zac stared at him a long moment. His expression told Wyll nothing of what was about to come out of his mouth. "Myranda."

Wyll frowned. "What about her?"

"Berent doesn't know she's with us."

"So?"

"Does he love her? I mean, really?"

Wyll gave it some thought. He'd never really gotten along with Berent, he was too arrogant and came off kind of controlling beneath his charming exterior. He tolerated him for his sister's sake because Berent always seemed to adore Myranda. "Yes, in his own way, I believe he does."

Zac smiled grimly. "Then this should work."

"What are you thinking?"

"The entire Newverse already thinks we kidnapped Meris, why wouldn't they believe we'd kidnap Berent Gaehts' wife?"

Wyll shook his head. "He wouldn't, though. He knows I'd never let anything happen to Myranda."

"No, you wouldn't."

Zac's expression became unreadable and Wyll went cold. Something shiny flicked out of Zac's pocket and into his right hand. Wyll had only a second to react, nearly breaking his ankle as he lurched off the stool. He maneuvered Zac into a joint lock, pressing his face to the countertop. He then grabbed Zac's right hand and brought it into view. A needle.

"What is this?"

"He'll never buy that you'd sit by and let me torture your sister."

He put more pressure on the locked arm until Zac cried out. "You have ten seconds to explain yourself before I break your arm. Or both of them."

"For show only, Wyll. I'd never really hurt her. But Berent needs to think I have and that I will. You gotta be taken out of the equation before he'd even remotely believe it."

Zac mule kicked Wyll in the left knee. With a sharp scream, Wyll stumbled back, losing his grip on Zac's wrists. And then Zac was on him, knocking him to the floor. There was a brief struggle before he felt the tiny pinprick of pain.

Zac watched Wyll as his body went still, the drug taking effect despite his efforts to fight. "I'm sorry, Lieutenant."

"What have... you...?"

"Don't worry. It's only a semi-paralytic. I can't have you trying to stop me from doing what needs to be done."

Wyll's hearing was going fuzzy, as if someone had stuffed cotton into his ears. His vision, too, was greying out, Zac's features becoming indistinct as he frowned down at him. His heartbeat began to slow and his breathing became shallow. He feared they would both stop altogether, but, so far, his heart was still pumping, and a slow stream of air was keeping his blood oxygenated.

He couldn't move his head already, but his bleary eyes could still follow Zac's every movement. The Egalian gave him an apologetic look, saying something Wyll couldn't decipher before using his vid-phone to send a message.

Zac leaned in closer. "I won't let anything happen to her. Please forgive me."

But Wyll didn't feel very forgiving. All he could feel was helpless. Betrayed. Enraged.

Above all, he felt rage.

CHAPTER 7 – ALAZAR

Her voice was so very far away. As hard as he tried, he couldn't make it come any closer and he knew he'd be lost if he didn't make it back to her. Why was he so drawn to this woman? She had done nothing to indicate he was anything more than a means to an end to her, had she? No. She was still in love with a dead man.

A man who was dead because of him. It was his fault, after all, just not as she had first thought. He needed to tell her the truth. He needed her to know the reason for her fiancé's death.

"Alazar, can you hear me?"

Yes, he wanted to say. Yes, I hear you. But he was too far from himself. Please keep talking. Keep me here.

"Please, God, let him live."

Was she praying for him? His heart constricted with this new, unfamiliar feeling. No one had prayed for him in a long, long time.

Meris.

"Alazar, please open your eyes. Please, God, just let him look at us."

I want to. I want to stay, would do anything to stay. For you. With you.

"Open your eyes, Darius."

She'd never said his name before.

He had to come back. He tried, but it was like pushing through sand.

Meris. Keep talking. Keep calling me back. Help me.

He was so tired. The sand was all around him, inside him. It *was* him. There was no way he was going to make it.

"We need you, Darius. *I* need you."

She needed him.

He had to push toward the surface. She needed him to push through. She needed him.

"Please, Darius. Please come back."

He was trying. He would make it back. He would. For her.

There was light. He pushed toward it. And finally, finally, the sand sifted away and he opened his eyes.

"Meris?"

CHAPTER 8 – MERIS

Meris checked her vid-phone for the fourteenth time. Wyll still hadn't responded to her message, which was... odd. Nothing from Zac, either.

"Myranda, has Wyll contacted you yet?"

She kept her voice low not to disturb Alazar, who had fallen asleep again. He seemed to be resting peacefully now that his fever had broken. He had managed to open his eyes and say her name an hour earlier but was too exhausted to maintain consciousness for long and had sank into a more natural sleep soon after. Her concern now was for Wyll; it wasn't like him to ignore them.

Myranda looked up from her tablet and shook her head. A tightness in her forehead and jaw betrayed how worried she was as well. "Neither has Zac."

"Do you know where they are?"

"No." Myranda's lips pressed into a thin line. "It was part of Wyll's plan. We weren't supposed to be able to give up their location if we got picked up by law enforcement or Berent's people. They don't know where we are, either, for the same reason." She went back to typing on her tablet, adding to the account she had written about discovering her husband's treachery and everything that has happened since.

Meris made a noncommittal sound. She wasn't sure where they were, either. Leo had taken them to some sort of farming community she had never heard of. Scania Farms claimed to be the provider of the best dairy in all Sindria, yet she couldn't think of a single instance of buying anything with their name on it. How Leo found it and arranged for them to stay at this abandoned cottage along the lush Helsing Sea coastline while Alazar recuperated was a mystery.

Leo turned from the window he'd been staring out of in the small living room and faced the two women. "Something has happened to them, hasn't it? They've been arrested, or- or-"

"Don't say that!" Myranda's voice cut through the dingy room. "They probably just had to go dark for a while."

"But they missed their check-in. They didn't even respond to Miss Brand's message about Mr. Alazar."

"Meris," she automatically corrected, though neither seemed to be listening.

"I know that, Leo," Myranda replied irritably. She set the tablet aside on a small wooden side table and picked at a loose embroidery thread on the navy blue throw pillow she held in her lap, on the surprisingly comfy couch on which she was seated next to Meris.

The fire Leo had built in the fieldstone fireplace to take the chill off the cool coastal air as it sliced through the drafty cottage crackled busily and cast golden flickers on the hearth. Meris glanced over as an ember popped out from under the fire-screen and rolled much too closely to Alazar's cot. She jumped up and kicked the red ember back onto the hearth then stomped out the smoldering spot on the edge of the musty blue blanket they'd covered him with.

Alazar stirred and reached for her. His fingertips traced the back of her hand as if trying to get her attention. But when she turned more toward him, he opened his eyes and stared at his surroundings in confusion. He seemed to relax a little when his gaze found Leo at the window. He then turned his head and saw Myranda on the couch at the foot of his bed.

Then he turned his eyes upon her. She couldn't pretend she didn't see the light that sparked to life in them or ignore the pain it caused deep in her gut. She forced a smile. "Welcome back, Alazar. How are you feeling?"

The light in his eyes dimmed slightly at her formal tone. Another twinge of guilt twisted inside her. Her smile faltered.

"Where are we?"

"Leo, you want to take this one?"

The Sendrassan man turned to Alazar and smiled ruefully. "Miss Brand- Meris seems to think I've taken us to the literal middle of nowhere."

"She's not too far off," Myranda scoffed, still picking at the loose thread.

"Don't worry, Mr. Alazar. Suffice it to say we're safer here than anywhere else I can think of."

Alazar shifted, trying to sit up. Meris put a hand on his shoulder. "I'm not so sure you should try that yet."

He gritted his teeth and pushed against her, apparently determined to sit up or split his incision open again, whichever came first. "We are wasting time here. Why aren't we at a Nexus Hub already?"

Meris and Leo shot a look at Myranda, who frowned tightly. "We can't," she told him. "Berent beat us to the press, remember? The whole Newverse thinks you, Wyll, Zac and Leo led the attacks on the Stell-Ore employees."

He stared at her a long moment. "I thought that had been a dream. I've had... so many dreams lately."

"Sorry, but this is no dream." Myranda twirled the thread, which Meris now noticed was a deep red, in a circle around her finger. "We were hoping Wyll and Zac would have an idea what to do next, but we... lost contact with them." The thread broke. She rolled it off her finger to fall to the floor.

Alazar flipped the musty blanket off himself and pulled out his IV needle. He paused a moment before pushing himself up and swinging his long legs over the side to sit on the edge of the bed. Meris placed a hand on his shoulder again to steady him. He was breathing rapidly and looked like he was going to collapse.

"What are you doing?"

"One... we need to... keep moving." He was out of breath that easily. "Two... I need... to use the facilities."

She felt her face flush. "Oh. Well, luckily, this place has actual plumbing."

Myranda stood up. "I'm his doctor, I'll help him."

"But I'm a guy, I'll give him a hand." Leo approached his boss, but then stopped cold. "Oh, eww, not literally though, sir."

"Thank you, Leo, that makes this so much less awkward." Alazar frowned, but Meris could see laughter in his striking blue eyes.

She stepped aside and let Leo help Alazar to his feet and out of the room. Once they had disappeared into the bathroom, one of the only three other rooms in the cottage, she turned to Myranda. "He can barely sit up or stand. What are we supposed to do if Berent and his people attack us? We can't keep him safe if we're being shot at."

"You and Leo will have to fight. I'll protect my patient."

Meris frowned at the idea of having to hurt someone to protect the others and herself. Even though she had taken a gun when they were trying to flee Stell-Ore, she had made certain that she was firing over the enemy's head. She honestly didn't know what she'd do if she were put in the position where she had to fight. She prayed it never came to that.

"But what do we do now? What is the plan?"

Myranda tilted her head back and exhaled noisily, something Meris had seen Wyll do when stressed. "I don't know, Meris. Why don't you tell us what the plan is? You're the one who started this whole crusade to begin with."

"Wait, what?" Anger bit at her tongue, goading her to lash out. Instead, she reined it in as best she could. "I did not start anything. Berent and his men did. All I wanted was to expose the truth. Do you think I planned to be on the run with the man I saw murder my fiancé, my friend – who is the sister of the man who killed him *and* the wife of the man who ordered it done – and the man I originally accused of being behind it all? This –" she flicked out a hand to indicate their surroundings, "is not where I pictured myself today."

Okay, so maybe she didn't rein it in very well after all.

"And you think I did?" Myranda scoffed. "Do you think any of the rest of us did? But this is where we are. And this is also where we can't stay. Alazar is right about that."

She took a breath to calm down. Fighting among themselves would solve nothing. "Granted, but I don't know what we can do instead. We need Wyll and Zac. As much as I hate to admit that."

"Wyll is not the enemy, Mer. Neither is Alazar or the others. I know this whole thing is hard, but I thought we were past that now."

"I – I am. It's just that when I look at them, I can't help but remember how I felt about them before I knew the truth. It's all still jumbled up in there together. And I don't know what to do with that yet."

The two men came back into the living room. Alazar flicked a glance at Meris before addressing Myranda. "How long since the last contact with them?"

Myranda was chewing on her thumb's cuticle. "Not since midnight. They missed their scheduled check-in time. Meris sent a buzz to Wyll then to let him know about your setback, so we expected him to respond to that, at least. Neither one of them has answered our buzzes or calls since. That was half an hour ago."

"Then we have to proceed under the assumption that they've been compromised somehow."

"But sir-"

"I know no one wants to think about this, Leo." Alazar stepped away from the Sendrassan and supported himself against the fireplace mantle, giving Myranda a sympathetic look. "But we can't hide out forever. We need to come forward, now."

"How? We'd never make it through the next big town. Have you forgotten that everyone in all seven colony-planets is out for our blood?"

Alazar shook his head. "No, Meris. Not our blood - mine. And you're going to give it to them."

Leo and Myranda started speaking at once. Meris simply stared for an extended moment before she had to ask, "What are you talking about?"

"You bring me in, tell them everything that really happened and hand me over. Of course, they won't want to believe you at first, but they'll have no choice but to investigate your claims. They will still put me on trial, I'm sure, but Berent has nothing to tie me to any of this. What was my motive supposed to have been for killing my crew? And for killing the rest of my employees – because they rioted against me? Did I simply go mad? If so, then why in the worlds would anyone have supported me? His whole argument will fall apart if the Council starts pulling the right thread. But before I make my case in the court of law, I'm going to wage my war in the court of public opinion."

Meris exchanged looks with each of them, then a smile stretched her lips as his plan fell into place in her mind.

"Meris, do you still have available memory on your vid-phone?"

Her smile broadened. "Yes, Darius, I do."

CHAPTER 9 – MERIS

Alazar looked her in the eye. "Ready?"

Meris glanced at her vid-phone screen once more to make sure the camera was centered before looking back at him. "Ready when you are."

He was perfectly framed in the camera, his wounds unmistakably visible in the morning's natural light flooding the dining area of the little cottage's kitchen. The white plaster wall behind him provided a neutral backdrop. The wooden corner nook bench on which he sat provided little comfort, but he had said that was the least of his priorities.

He nodded and cleared his throat, then straightened his posture as much as possible. Meris tapped the icon to start recording, then gave him a nod. He took a deep breath. "My name is Darius Alazar. As you all must know by now, I am being accused of the terrible crimes - the atrocities - that occurred at my company, Stell-Ore Mining. The first of these atrocities was the senseless and brutal killing of the crew of Cartage 15, one of the best crews I had in my employ."

He paused for a moment as Meris' hand started to shake. A tear fell down her face, but she wiped it away, steadied her hand and nodded for him to continue. "In the aftermath of that tragedy, a very brave young woman took it upon herself to infiltrate my headquarters with the intent of accusing me of the crime. I will ever be grateful to this young woman, the fiancée of my crew chief, Ellias Gammett, one of the casualties of the Cartage 15 massacre. Her name is Meris Brand, and she is filming this video. Say hello, Miss Brand."

She didn't know he was going to do that, but she immediately saw his plan. She wiped her tears some more and turned the vid-phone camera toward herself. "Hello. I want to put an end to the rumors that Darius Alazar and his supporters kidnapped me and are holding me against my will. This is not true. I am here by my own choice because I now know the truth behind my fiancé's death. Please, listen to what Alazar has to say; it is the truth." She glanced back to see him smiling. He nodded that he was ready to resume. She switched the camera back to him.

"Thank you, Miss Brand. I am grateful to her for uncovering the truth behind the Cartage 15 massacre. She confronted me with footage immortalized by the same vid-phone with which this message is being recorded. In this footage, I saw a member of my own elite security staff purposely putting a bullet into Ellias Gammett's skull, murdering him in front of Miss Brand's very eyes. I cannot imagine the horror and grief this act has caused her." He looked past the camera to her, his eyes soft and full of empathy. She felt more tears falling.

"However, this footage proved that the deaths of this crew were not the result of an accident, an equipment malfunction, nor the result of the crew chief's own actions, as some suggested. Ellias Gammett did not get a brain-bug and go mad; he and his crew were not infected by any pathogen picked up on Thalassa. This is what the young Lieutenant who led the attack on this crew was told. He was made to believe that he was carrying out a security protocol in place to ensure that no off-world diseases ever make it back to Sindria, or any of the other colony-planets. This Lieutenant is Wyll Meiryg. He received this order from Commander Hauher, who is the commanding officer over all soldiers on my security staff.

"Lieutenant Meiryg, Meris Brand and other members of my staff supported me when the real culprit was revealed to be Berent Gaehts, the cartage crew chief who usurped my position as Head of Operations of Stell-Ore Mining. Berent Gaehts framed me for these crimes, attacked me and imprisoned me in what is not-so-affectionately known as The Hole – one of the many training facilities within the Stell-Ore Securities Compound that was not under my direct supervision."

He paused, his gaze going inward. "Had I known what that place was, how it was used, I would have seen to it personally that it was demolished. This is a place of isolation, where I was beaten and tortured by Commander Hauher, several of his soldiers and even Berent Gaehts himself."

"Many of you will say that this message is simply a delaying tactic, an attempt to muddy the waters in order to save my own skin from the Chamber. I understand why you will think this. I can only hope to change your mind with the truth."

This was the part Meris was dreading most. He had refused to tell her in advance what he was about to reveal, and her mind raced with the possibilities. All he would say was that she would see why it really was his fault after all, even if he never pulled the trigger.

"Miss Brand does not know what I am about to tell you. None of my companions do. When I have finished, I will go to the nearest Law Enforcement station, where I will turn myself over to the authorities so that this whole story will be forced to be aired in open court. I will stand before the Council and answer for the part I did play in this tragedy, but I will also defend my innocence of the deeds themselves. Berent Gaehts and Commander Hauher are the ones who are guilty of these crimes. I was merely the one who unwittingly incited them."

He took another deep, steadying - or perhaps cleansing? – breath. He then looked her in the eye and said: "I had drafted Berent Gaehts termination papers. I had asked Ellias and several others from 16 who had expressed interest to relocate to the refinery in the wake of the retirement of several long-term employees. Ellias would have had command of the refinery crew, of Berent's men. The rest were to be merged with 15 – under Dusa's command – and a few other crews. It was going to serve as my wedding gift to Ellias Gammett and Meris Brand, as it would mean he would be staying on Sindria instead of traveling to mine the Bolidium."

She couldn't hold back the tears, and a sob wracked her body, making her nearly drop the vid-phone. He reached across the table and took her hand in his, gently steadying the camera and offering solace in one gesture. She would have had her wish; she would have had Ellias with her always. It would have been perfect.

And it had been taken from her. Berent had robbed Ellias and her of their future. But wait...if he'd been fired, how was it he'd been there the day she infiltrated Stell-Ore?

"When did you tell him?"

Alazar winced. "That morning, right before 15 set out for Thalassa. He was going to tell you when he got home. He wanted to marry you as soon as he returned."

She was shaking so hard she could barely keep the camera on him. "No, I meant Berent. When did you tell Berent he had been fired and your plan for his crew?"

He looked down at the top of the table. "I didn't. I don't know how he put it together, but no, I hadn't gotten the chance to tell him. I was going to that day, but then the... incident on Thalassa happened – what I at first thought was just an accident, and I was so busy with the follow up, the investigation, I didn't even have time to think about Berent. Until you showed up at Stell-Ore and he tried to throw you out once you'd accused me but, conveniently, before I could see the video on your phone for myself. You don't know this, but his supporters attacked me when you ran, at the same time he attacked you. That was the moment the coup was struck. I got away for a time, with Wyll's help. But Berent had already seized control of my security systems and his soldiers found me... I was outnumbered. It was not a fight I could win."

"They were friends... for over ten years. They shared an apartment for five years. How could he have just... murdered him so coldly like this? All over a job?"

He looked away. "I should have seen something like this coming."

"How? How could you have predicted this?"

"The reason I was firing him, it was because of the rumors."

She furrowed her brow. "What rumors?"

CHAPTER 10 – ZAC

The first thing Zac noticed was that it was getting easier to breathe. What he had done to Wyll – as a subordinate and as a friend – was unforgivable. Telling his Lieutenant he hadn't intended to attack him until he found himself doing so would be no excuse. Especially since he overpowered Wyll a second time to finish the job. He could be court martialed for this.

If they survived this thing, that is.

When he could collect himself enough to stop his hands from shaking, he composed a buzz to Myranda and pushed the SEND button. Now all he had to do was wait. He ran his fingers through his short, light brown hair and took another deep breath. If Myranda didn't agree to this, the whole plan would fall through and Wyll would kill him. Or at least kick his butt.

Two minutes later, his vid-phone emitted a sharp beep and rumbled with vibration. He startled so hard a muscle twinged in his neck and he snatched up the device with a self-chiding grunt. The message was exactly what he wanted to see:

About time you answered. We thought you'd been caught. Alazar was ready to martyr himself. Your plan might work... On our way.

Zac smiled and turned his attention to Wyll's sprawled form on the pale blue carpet. Wyll's face was devoid of expression, of course, since his facial muscles were also paralyzed, but the look in his eyes was murderous. Zac couldn't afford to think about what was going through the Lieutenant's mind now.

He didn't know where Myranda and the others were and had no idea how long it would take her to get here. Since he and Wyll arrived last night, he had managed to get some food into himself, but he hadn't slept more than an hour or two and was in dire need of a shower. There should be time to get properly cleaned up before Myranda arrived.

He entered Jenna's small bathroom, a clean but stark room, and opened the linen closet to get a towel. He couldn't help but laugh when he took one off the top of the stack. "Guess you had a girly streak in you after all."

The towel became a bright pink blur as tears filled his eyes. He balled it up and pressed his face into it, letting the tears come. He owed her this. There was no one else to really mourn her, and only a hastily dug grave in Leo's back yard to memorialize her.

"I'm so sorry, Jenna." His voice was a hoarse whisper. How did everything keep going from bad to worse? How had life gotten so turned upside-down so fast?

Berent Gaehts had a lot to answer for.

Once he composed himself again, he stripped down and opened the shower stall. Here, too, were little hints of Jenna's spunky personality, in the form of a wash mitt shaped like a skunk with the words 'Funk Buster' written across its belly in neon green letters, and bottles of the apple-scented body wash and shampoo she always used. He turned the showerhead on and stepped in, letting the hot water pelt his body.

He opened the bottle of body wash and inhaled the scent, remembering the first time he had met Jenna. She had had a proverbial chip on her shoulder the size of a city block, owing, he suspected, to her tomboyish looks and lower-class upbringing. Not to mention the fact that she was an Egalian female trying to fit in on a squad of mostly Sindrian males. She had seemed relieved to find out that Zac, too, was an off-worlder, and that there were many others in the Stell-Ore Security Compound, including their Lieutenant.

But that didn't mean that she'd ever stopped trying to prove herself the equal of him or any other man in the unit. She'd even punched him in the face the first time he'd accidentally called her 'kid.' But once he explained that that was his nickname for his little sister, and that she reminded him of her so much, she asked him to forgive her. She then said not to let it happen again, though, or she'd punch him harder next time.

That was pretty much the moment he'd adopted her as his responsibility and vowed to protect her.

He hoped, when he met her in the Hereafter, she would forgive him for failing.

After 'busting the funk' off himself, he wrapped the pink towel around his waist and grabbed his clothes. The lingering stench of smoke from the explosion he and Wyll had staged combined with two days of wear and tear on the run wafted up from them. He frowned. There was a washer-dryer in the kitchen if he remembered correctly.

But that meant walking past Wyll.

Clenching his jaw, he strode across the floor straight to the kitchen without sparing a glance for his Lieutenant. He didn't want to see how his eyes seemed to stare at him with rage, no matter where he stood. He threw his clothes into the washer-dryer and hit the start button. The small, cube-shaped appliance filled with the chemical-laced steam that cleansed the garments in a matter of minutes. The cycle then changed over to dry them in an equally short time.

In less than five minutes, he was dressed again. When he could take it no longer, he turned around.

Wyll was staring at him again.

"Don't look at me like that." He tossed the pink towel across Wyll's face and stormed out of the room.

CHAPTER 11 – MERIS

Myranda paced in a tight circuit like a caged beast. Meris sympathized with her anxiety and eagerness to be off, but Alazar wasn't convinced to go along with their plan. Not yet.

"I can't believe you're not chomping at the bit here – this is a way to draw him out and keep you out of chains, and you're – what? – second-guessing it? This is insane!" Myranda's fists were balled at her sides, and it looked like it was taking every ounce of self-control to keep from punching Alazar out and forcing him to go along with it.

"I think she's right," Meris said. "If we can do this without giving you up to the Enforcers, then we should at least try it."

Myranda gave her a grateful smile. "Just give this a chance before you go off and martyr yourself." Her tone was borderline pleading.

Alazar's jaw muscles twitched as he mulled it over. But his arms remained crossed over his chest and his eyes were cast toward the floor between his bed and the hearth. It would be a miracle if he relented. Meris knelt next to him.

"Darius, please. If this works – and that's a big if, I admit – but if it does work, we will have Berent in our hands. We can force him to tell the truth, for the whole Newverse to see." She placed a hand on his knee and tilted into his line of sight, forcing him to look at her. "Your message can still go out, sure, but you wouldn't have to turn yourself in for something you didn't do."

His eyes locked onto hers and her gut twisted again. Before her was a man willing to risk the Chamber to expose the truth and get justice for her murdered fiancé, and she was manipulating him like some conniving vamp because she suspected he cared for her. She felt like throwing up.

"We had a plan, Meris." His voice was soft and low, weary. "One that would keep the rest of you out of the Council's hands. I cannot guarantee anyone's safety or freedom if we abandon it now."

"I know. But we're not asking you to. We're asking you to trust that Berent's own nature will work against him, that Myranda and Zac and I can take care of the rest. If it doesn't work, we still have your plan to fall back on."

He took a slow breath. "There are too many moving parts. I don't like it."

Myranda threw her hands up and growled in frustration. Alazar raised a hand to ask her to hear him out. "But it could work. If Zac can sell Berent on his story, and if you can pretend you don't know what kind of monster you married, we have a chance. But I can't be anywhere near it. If he even suspects I know about this, he'll bolt."

Meris shook her head. "We're not leaving you here alone."

He covered her hand with one of his. "Leo can stay, if you wish. It will be down to him to get my message out on the Nexus anyway, if Zac's plan fails."

She chewed her lower lip and felt anxiety crawling around in her stomach. It was too much, all of it, too much to keep bearing. If it could be over, and without losing him to the Council... She turned to Leo.

"Will you stay with him?"

Leo nodded but there was fear behind his eyes. "Of course."

Alazar squeezed her hand. "It's settled, then." She turned back to see him smiling sadly at her. "I'll see you soon." Her heart broke at the look on his face. He turned to Myranda. "I'll see you both very soon. And I hope this will all be over when I do."

Myranda looked him in the eye a long moment. Then she nodded. "Thank you." Her gaze flicked to Meris. "Come on, Zac's expecting us."

CHAPTER 12 – MERIS

Zac frowned as he opened the door to Jenna's apartment. "Are the others okay?"

"Fine," Myranda answered as they entered the small, tidy living space.

Meris looked past him to see Wyll lying immobile on the floor. She gasped. "What happened?"

"Meris, it's fine-"

She shoved by and dropped to her knees next to Wyll. A bright pink towel covered his face. She pulled it away with a trembling hand. Wyll's eyes slowly closed and then opened again. She turned back to Zac and Myranda. "He's alive?"

Zac nodded. "Semi-paralytic. Like Berent used on you."

Meris narrowed her eyes. A bruise was purpling up on the side of Zac's face. She gestured to the same spot on her own face then pointed to him and asked, "What happened there?"

He blushed and looked at the floor. "I, uh, sorta didn't tell him my plan first."

"What?" She flicked a glance at Myranda, who simply pressed her lips into a thin line and shook her head incredulously. Meris turned back to Wyll. "I know this is frustrating – believe me – but it's our best shot. Hopefully, it will be over soon. We're going to get him."

Wyll's eyes blinked slowly twice. She frowned. "No? You don't think so?"

His eyes burned with rage and frustration. He blinked twice again, then closed his eyes. She touched a hand to his arm. Turning away, she spoke to the others. "Okay, Zac, we're all in it now. What's next?"

Instead of letting him answer, Myranda turned to face him. She took a short breath and said, "Don't hold back."

He nodded and before Meris could guess what was coming, punched Myranda in the face. In time with Myranda's grunt of pain, Meris yelled, "What are you doing?"

Myranda straightened and faced him again, just in time to meet his backhand to the other side of her face. She staggered back against the armchair, blood gushing from her nose and split lip. Zac grimaced but readied a fist all the same.

Meris gasped. This had gone too far. As Zac advanced toward Myranda once more, Meris lunged toward him and jabbed her fingers into the healing HEL-gun wound in his side.

Zac shouted and backfisted her as he whirled away from Myranda. With a yelp, Meris went sprawling backward onto the carpeted floor. Zac immediately dropped to his knees next to her.

"I'm sorry! You surprised me and I just... reacted." He reached a hand toward her but withdrew it when she flinched. "I'm sorry."

"What is all this? No one said anything about paralyzing Wyll or beating up Myranda! I thought she was just going to be tied up so we could lure him out."

"We are," Myranda answered, cradling the side of her face. "This is how we do it. Though I thought you had filled Wyll in instead of attacking him. Seriously, Zac..." She turned from chastising him to address Meris. "Check on him, will you? He's probably very confused and angry right now."

Zac dipped his head, looking at the floor. "He hates me. And I can't blame him. I didn't entrust him with the details... I just blindsided him."

Meris went back to Wyll and laid two fingers to his throat. His pulse was slow but steady. She smiled and placed her hand on his chest, feeling the slow rise and fall of his breathing. "Trust me, I know how unpleasant this is. But it will wear off soon."

"Uh, Meris," Zac said, "if you're ready, we need to get set up."

She patted Wyll's chest and went over to take the tablet Myranda was handing to her. Wyll was lying in the open space between the kitchen counter and dining area, next to the living room, which spanned the length of both the other rooms. The front door was in the living room, on the end closest to the kitchen, not the dining room. The best place to set up the camera would be the dining room table. She moved one of the plastex chairs out from the steel table and sat, lining up the camera on Myranda's tablet to show Wyll and the front door. It was strange being in Jenna's home like this without the Egalian girl with them. It felt like a total invasion of privacy, even though she knew the dead no longer cared about such things. All the same, she felt extremely out of place and awkward. *Sorry, Jenna...*

"Okay, all set," she told Zac.

"Good. Myranda, I'll need to tie you to this chair over here." Zac moved one of the living room chairs – a leatherex armchair with a bold pink and white floral print – into position.

Myranda sat in the chair and Zac used some zip-ties to loosely secure her hands and feet to the chair. "You know, under other circumstances, having a lovely woman willing to let me tie her up could be fun." Zac winked at her.

Myranda laughed. "In your dreams, Zac."

He grinned broadly. "Count on it."

"Eww." Meris and Myranda both said, and they both ended up laughing.

"Hold that thought," Zac told Myranda. "I've got a phone call to make. I'll need your vid-phone."

Myranda jutted her chin toward the counter where her vid-phone was lying. Zac grabbed it and came back. He held the vid-phone up to frame a picture of Myranda. "Say moon-cheese," he told her. "And try to act like you hate me."

She smiled sweetly. "That shouldn't be too hard."

"Ha ha. Ready?" She nodded and made her expression look scared and angry. "Perfect. One, two, three..." He took the photo.

When he was done, Meris made sure the loops around her friend's hands and feet were loose enough for her to slip free easily when needed. Zac was composing the buzz to accompany the photo. With all at the ready, Meris took up her position at the table, pausing long enough to bend down and squeeze Wyll's shoulder reassuringly.

"Don't worry," she told him before getting into place.

Zac sent the buzz then set the vid-phone on the counter. Seconds ticked by. Then the phone finally emitted a chime and buzzed.

"Show time," Zac said before answering it.

Meris tapped the RECORD button on the tablet and settled in to watch the plan play out.

Berent's deep voice filled the air. "Who are you and what have you done to my wife?"

"Retract your accusations against Darius Alazar."

Berent laughed. "Do you think kidnapping Myranda is going to help your boss? All it does is show I'm right about him and his supporters. You're all monsters."

Myranda fixed a glare so hateful on Zac that Meris almost forgot she was pretending. "Berent, don't do anything he says."

"Where are Miss Brand and my wife's... rabble-rousing brother?"

Zac panned the vid-phone to show Wyll's prone figure. "Out of the equation, for the moment."

"Why, if he's on your side? I'm assuming by 'for the moment' that means you didn't kill him, which is a pity-"

"What did you just say?" Myranda's voice sounded genuinely appalled.

"I'm sorry, honey, but Wyll turned people against me so the real monster, Alazar, could escape justice. If he were dead, the truth could finally be told and all those lives avenged." He affected a sympathetic tone of voice. "Hard to hear, I know, but it's true."

"He's not dead. Just incapacitated while I had a little chat with your wife."

Berent sighed. "Looks like I'll have to kill both of you when I see you, then. But don't worry, Myranda, I'll at least make Wyll's death quick. Not sure I can say the same for this guy."

Zac smiled. "You see, sweetness? I told you that you married a monster."

A tear dripped from Myranda's chin. She closed her eyes and looked down at the floor. A moment later, her shoulders shook with quiet crying.

"You didn't fully answer my question," Berent went on. "Where is Meris Brand?"

"You don't need to worry about her. All you need to worry about is what I'll have to do if you don't recant your accusation against Darius Alazar."

"Oh, 'what you have to do?' Which is what? Kill my wife?"

Zac shook his head and put Myranda in the vid-phone's frame again. "No, no – I'm going to torture her. And you are going to watch every second of it. Unless you recant and confess to what you've done."

"Berent, please!" Myranda begged, pretending to struggle with her bonds. "Please don't let him hurt me again."

"Myranda, honey, listen to me: you are going to be fine. This coward won't lay another hand on you."

A laser dot appeared on Zac's back. Meris shouted, "Zac, get down!"

CHAPTER 13 – ZAC

Zac dropped to the ground just as the window behind him shattered. Searing pain ripped through his back. Meris and Myranda screamed.

"Meris, get Myranda and help Wyll out of here!"

He couldn't see, but knew Myranda would have already slipped the zip-ties off her wrists and ankles as planned. The two of them would need to carry Wyll out. Shot in the back, there was no way he could help them with that now.

"I'm not leaving you!" Meris was right next to him now, trying to help him to his feet. Another airbolt shot flew over their heads, breaking the dishes on one of the kitchen shelves.

"Make sure Myranda's free."

She grunted in frustration but started across the room. "Stay down!" Zac shouted to her as more shots tore through the apartment.

The door to the apartment came flying open, Berent behind it. Zac tried to get up, but his legs weren't obeying him. Panic threatened to overwhelm him. If he couldn't get up and run, Berent would end him here and now. Zac twisted around further and fumbled for the handgun in his leg holster. Meris and Myranda stood between him and Berent.

"Get down!"

The women started to move but Berent brought his gun up into Meris' face. She froze. With a wordless cry, Myranda pushed her aside as he fired.

Myranda dropped like a broken toy.

Zac screamed and opened fire at the Riekan. One bullet hit him square in the chest, but he was apparently still wearing the body armor he stole from the security compound. The second bullet bit deep into his right shoulder and he lowered the airbolt gun with a yowl of pain. Meris flew at him, clambering up on his back and grappling to get her arm under his chin.

Berent turned side to side quickly, clawing at her arms trying to dislodge her. She changed tactic and dug her fingers into his bullet wound. He growled through gritted teeth and slammed backward, pinning Meris between him and the wall. He slammed her against it twice more before she let go and rolled to the floor.

Zac shot again but Berent dodged, running out the door instead. Sirens were approaching. He could hear Meris crying and calling out Myranda's name.

The tablet and vid-phone. If the police saw the videos, they'd believe Zac really had kidnapped the two women. He glanced around. The tablet was still set up on the table. At least it would have recorded Berent's attack. He couldn't get to it, but the vid-phone was on the floor next to him. He reached for it, his fingertips barely making contact. "Come on," he growled. But then his fingers found purchase on the screen and he was able to pull it close.

"Meris, how is she?"

She was sobbing too hard to answer. His heart nearly stopped. No. She can't be dead. "Wyll, if you can hear me, you've got to start moving."

Zac craned his head back to see his Lieutenant still lying immobile. He turned back to Meris. "Meris, you gotta get Wyll out of here and get the vid-phone and tablet back to Alazar."

He held the vid-phone out to her; she didn't look up. The sirens were getting closer. "Meris! You have to get out of here!"

She looked at him then. It took a moment but recognition of what he was telling her finally dawned on her face. She hurried to him and took the device. Tears streamed down her face.

"The tablet's still on the table. Take the vid-phone and it and get Wyll out. Get to Alazar."

"No, you're coming with us." She tugged on his arm again.

"I can't – I can't move my legs." Tears came involuntarily. "I'm sorry. It wasn't supposed to happen like this."

She started crying again, words that sounded like prayer coming brokenly between sobs. But then a change came over her expression, like a thought had occurred to her. "Wait, let me see." She pushed his arm, rolling him over. With a relieved laugh she said, "It's just a Stinger."

"What?" His heart pounded as hoped flooded him.

"Yeah, let me just dig it out." She grunted lightly as she pulled the device from his back. "There."

She held the bloody object for him to see. Shaped sort of like a corkscrew, the Stinger had a needle that penetrates the target's skin to hold it in place while the body of the device delivered a neuro-disruptor charge. The charge rendered the victim paralyzed from the point of entry down until removed.

"Oh, thank you, God." Already, sensation was returning to his lower body. He ignored the pins-and-needles feeling and rose to his hands and feet. He touched her arm and gave her a grateful smile. "Get Wyll, I'll get Myranda."

"Zac..." Meris gave him a look, shaking her head as tears slid down her face.

She can't be dead. What would Wyll do without her? He closed his eyes a moment, then lowered his voice so Wyll wouldn't hear. "We can't leave her here."

"We have to." She shivered. "Maybe this way Berent will go down for her even if we can't prove his involvement with Stell-Ore." She looked over her shoulder as the sirens grew louder. "Come on, they're almost here."

Tears blurred his vision. "This isn't right." He shook his head, surrendering. "Let's get Wyll and get out of here."

She sniffed and nodded and the two of them lifted Wyll to his feet. He couldn't look at him. The shock and grief would be evident in his eyes, as well as the helplessness of being unable to even go to his sister and touch her hand in one last parting. But there was no time, even if Wyll had been mobile. Zac did his best to turn them all away as they passed her body on the way out of the apartment.

This isn't right...
Wyll is going to hate me.

CHAPTER 14 – MERIS

She and Zac heaved Wyll into the transporter. "I'm so sorry, Wyll, I'm so sorry," Zac said for the fourth time as he and Meris climbed in.

"Zac, get us out of here!"

He wiped the heels of his hands across his eyes and sniffled but strapped into the pilot's seat and powered up the vehicle. "Hang on."

She sat on the carpeted floor, her back against the vehicle's steel side panel, since they had laid Wyll across the seats. She wiped her own tears away and reached up to take his hand in hers. He couldn't move fully yet, but he did manage to turn his head away from her. She let go.

"It's my fault," she told him. "You said it yourself: I started this whole thing. First Jenna, and now –" She couldn't even say Myranda's name. Guilt like bile burned in her throat, leaving much the same bitter taste on her tongue. "Don't blame Zac. It's my fault, not his."

He shook his head, sobs wracking his body. He couldn't raise his hands to cover his face, so he just kept looking at the back of the seats. She hugged her arms around her knees and laid her forehead on them. Could someone cry forever, or would they eventually run out of tears?

Please forgive me, Lord. They're dead because of me. I thought I was doing the right thing by going to Stell-Ore, but if I hadn't, Jenna and Myranda would still be alive.

No one spoke for half an hour, though she could hear Zac's occasional sigh and Wyll's sniffling. Her own weeping had wrung everything from her, and she felt limp and drained like an empty canteen. Her eyelids were growing heavy and were just about to close when she heard thumping and a short, surprised cry. Her eyes flew open to see the seats empty.

"No!"

She sprang to her feet right as the transporter lurched sideways, knocking her back against the side panel. Her head struck a metal support bar and stars burst in her vision. The transporter lurched the opposite direction, sending her sprawling on the floor.

"Wyll! You're gonna kill us!" Zac's yell was full of panic.

She looked up to see Zac and Wyll fighting for control of the vehicle. Zac looked terrified. Wyll looked... devoid of emotion. She wasn't sure which scared her more. She pushed herself up and jumped onto Wyll's back, like she had Berent's. He cried out and tried to throw her off but didn't let go of the controls.

"No, don't-!"

Zac's sentence got cut off as the transporter slammed to the earth. Like a stone across water, the vehicle skipped across a field she barely glimpsed before being tossed against the ceiling. Three times they hit the ground before sliding to a halt near a huge fir tree whose branches had come to within inches of piercing their windscreen. She lay still for several minutes, trying to assess how badly she was hurt. Her head was bleeding from the gash in the back from the support bar, and from above her right temple from hitting the floor. Her forearms and knees were sore, but nothing felt broken.

With a groan, she rolled onto her back. Wyll stood glowering over her, fists balled and ready to strike. She threw her hands up and closed her eyes. "Don't!"

"Get up."

She peeked through one eye. He hadn't struck, but his fists were still readied. She sat up. He jerked her the rest of the way to her feet and shoved her toward the open door. She stumbled out of the transporter and collapsed on the scrubby, grassy ground. The transporter hissed and ticked, and the scent of torn earth and fir needles filled the air. A moment later, Wyll emerged, dragging a half-conscious Zac with him.

Zac's face was a mess of blood and contusions. He held himself only partially upright, his right arm clasped around his chest. Wyll threw him to the ground next to Meris.

"Which one of you was it?" He paced in front of them, breathing hard and glaring dangerously. "Who did this?"

She glanced at Zac to make sure he was okay then stood to face the angry Tudoryan. "Wyll, please, just take a moment-"

He shoved her, sending her flat on her bottom with a yelp. Zac jumped to his feet. "Leave her alone!"

Wyll punched at him, but Zac dodged at the last second. "Stop!" Her voice was swallowed up in the men's snarling at each other. She dragged herself up and stood between them, shoving a hand against each one's chest. "I said STOP!"

Wyll gave her a murderous glare but went still. Zac took a step backward and wiped blood from under his nose. She turned her back on him and faced Wyll head-on. "I already told you that if I hadn't come to Stell-Ore, none of this would have happened, so if you're looking for someone to blame, blame me."

Tears slipped from her eyes. Wyll scoffed and began pacing in front of her. His glare darted from her to Zac and then back. She moved with him to keep between the two men. "I don't know what else you want me to say. There are no words for what I've caused."

He got in her face. "I want to know who told Berent where we were." His voice was cold and quiet. "I want to know if it was both of you working together to betray us or if it was just one of you. Have you always been working for Berent, or did he turn you?" He stopped, his face inches from hers. "I want to know which one of you to *kill* for causing my sister's death." Tears broke free of his lashes and he swiped at them angrily. Then he shouted, "Which one of you?!"

She held her hands out in a futile placating gesture. "Wyll, please, step back. You're scaring me."

"You're not scared yet."

"Wyll, man, come on – it's us," Zac said, putting his hands on her shoulders and pulling her slightly away from their grief-maddened friend. "We would never do what you're suggesting. If I had known this could happen, I never would've – I never meant for this." He wiped away more blood and a stray tear. "Please believe me, we didn't do this."

Wyll was pacing again, but the worst of his fury seemed to have abated. "Then explain to me how he knew where we were. He couldn't have followed us to Jenna's from Leo's place, and he wouldn't have known we'd go there ahead of time. He didn't know her. So that only leaves one of you," he jabbed a finger at them.

She thought a moment. Berent, they now knew, was paranoid and unstable. She withdrew Myranda's vid-phone and tablet from her pockets and frowned at the cracked screens. "Do you think he would have...?" She held the devices up toward Wyll.

He froze for a moment, but then took the tablet and vid-phone from her. He knelt to set them face-down on the ground and popped off the back covers. She didn't know exactly what it was supposed to look like inside them, but his expression told her this was not it.

He ran a hand over his face. That was when she became aware of blood dribbling down from his forehead and swelling and discoloration around his right eye and cheek. None of them had come out of this unscathed. He gently picked up two tiny rectangular objects with a miniscule blinking green light embedded in a white plastex exterior, one from each device.

"Trackers," he said. With an angry growl, he crushed the objects in his hand and stood to fling the pieces across the field.

He dropped to his knees again, his fist pressed to his mouth as he stared at the disassembled devices. They all went still, no one daring to break the silent, tense moment. At length, Wyll reassembled the tablet and vid-phone then raised his eyes toward her. He quickly looked away again and stood to view the damaged transporter, pocketing the devices.

"Miss Brand – Meris... Zac..." He turned but didn't quite look them in the eye. "I don't know what to say... I don't know how to apologize for," he made a vague gesture, "everything. Please forgive me."

She exchanged a look with Zac. He nodded. She sighed with relief and turned back to Wyll. "We understand. Either one of us would have thought the same thing in your position. I just don't know if you can ever forgive me for starting this."

His shoulders slumped. "Berent would have done all of this whether you'd come to Stell-Ore to accuse Alazar or not. He's probably been planning this for months."

She shook her head, recalling what Alazar had told her. "Two weeks ago, rumors began circling among the cartage crews. Members of 16 were starting to wonder if Berent had picked up a brain-bug on Nevzaris, the last posting they had before they were due to relieve 15 on Thalassa. Something happened either on Nevzaris or on the way back, Alazar didn't tell me the full story. But whatever it was, it frightened Berent's crew."

Wyll and Zac stared at her. "Two weeks ago?" Wyll asked. "Two weeks ago, Berent's crew told Alazar they were afraid of him and thought he might have a brain-bug and he did *nothing*?"

She placed a hand on his bicep to keep him from getting riled up again. "No. None of them came forward. They were too afraid of Berent. Alazar heard it from Ellias the day before he was killed. Ellias had had his own concerns about Berent and questioned some of 16's crewmembers. They told him what happened, but wouldn't report it, so Ellias did." She had to stop and take a breath, trying to quell the grief and anger that swelled inside her.

"Alazar said he told Ellias he was going to have Berent quarantined and questioned the next morning. If it was true that he'd been infected – even if he hadn't, actually – Alazar was going to put Ellias in charge of 15 and 16 and move both crews to the Sindria plant so they wouldn't have to go off-world anymore."

"But Berent found out and somehow got Hauher to give me the order to take out 15 and use it as a ruse to incite an uprising against Alazar to jump-start his coup," Wyll guessed.

"Exactly. He had you kill him in front of me to get me to make the allegations against Alazar to justify. Ellias called me every day at the same time whenever off-world; Berent knew it. It was easy enough to manage, I'm sure. Whether he does have a brain-bug, or he's just gone insane the old-fashioned way, none of that matters. What matters is that we stick together, trust each other, and work together to bring him to justice."

Zac squeezed her shoulder. "You know I'm in. For Jenna and 15. And Myranda." He held out a hand to Wyll. "Together."

Wyll shook it and then took her hand in his. "For 15, Jenna, and Myranda." He turned back and surveyed the transporter. "Let's see if this thing can still fly."

He climbed into the pilot's seat and brought the engines rumbling back to life. She and Zac climbed in and strapped into the passenger seats. Wyll glanced back at them. "Hang on, this might be a bit bumpy."

The transporter lurched into the air, jerking around like an inebriated Earth-born after an Earth History Day celebration, before stabilizing its hover. The engines billowed a cloud of black smoke that washed over the hull as Wyll started them forward at a snail's pace. When no other smoke followed, he put them at full speed. She gave him the coordinates of the cottage and they sped away, the vehicle juddering like they were in a constant cloud of turbulence.

CHAPTER 15 – ALAZAR

Something had gone wrong. He could feel it. Zac should have called by now... or Meris... or Myranda or Wyll. "We should have heard from them long before now."

Leo looked up at him. He was splicing footage he'd copied from Meris' vid-phone in with the message Darius had recorded, getting it ready to blast throughout the whole Newverse. "Maybe it's just taking a little longer than they expected."

"No, I can feel it. Something went wrong." An almost electric fear coursed through his body. "We should leave. We can contact Meris and the others on the way, but it's not safe here anymore."

Leo tapped the screen a couple more times. "There. The video is ready. I'm uploading it to all social media sites now. But we really do need to get to a Nexus hub to get it out into the mainstream."

"Yes, of course. But it is out there now, yes?"

"Yep. And you can't stop the signal." The way he said this made if obvious he was quoting something, but Darius didn't get the reference.

Leo's chuckle and smile died out. "Guess you aren't a fan of classic Earth sci-fi."

"Leo. We. Need. To. Leave. Now. Did you not hear me?"

"Right. Yes, sorry, boss." He tucked the tablet into a pocket and came over to help him up off the couch.

"I need real clothes. I won't make it two feet out of the transporter without being noticed in these scrubs."

Leo went still. "Ah, crap... that's right," he said slowly.

"What's wrong?"

"Well...Zac and Wyll took the Stell-Ore PTV when we got you out of the hospital and Myranda and Meris took my transporter to meet up with them at Jenna's, so..."

"We don't have a vehicle."

"No. But we could probably borrow one. There were a few near the other empty cottages here that might still run." He cocked his head to one side. "It's not still considered stealing if we plan to give it back afterward, is it?"

"I don't think the law makes such distinctions, Leo. But we don't have a choice."

"Right. Well, then we might as well steal you some clothes, too, while we're at it. Let me check the closet in the bedroom."

He pushed himself away from Leo's support. "I will do that. You concentrate on getting us a way out of here."

"Got it. I'll just," he gestured toward the door. "I won't be far, if you need me."

He nodded to the little Sendrassan and picked his way down the short hallway to the bedroom. The bed was in the living room in front of the fireplace, where Myranda had insisted he be laid, so the small room looked empty and forlorn. He hobbled to the closet and opened the door. A chest of drawers and a rod of hanging clothes stood inside.

The clothes on the rod were women's dresses. He pulled open the top drawer. Women's undergarments. The rest of the drawers also held nothing but women's garments. He nearly laughed at the thought of disguising himself as a woman, but then he spied a couple of boxes tucked away in the corner.

"Here we are," he said, finding men's trousers and shirts in the first box.

He pulled out a plain, heavy-duty canvas work shirt and held it up against his body. It was a little wide through the torso and barely reached his hips but would have to do. The same with the trousers, too big around but not quite long enough. These predated fiber compression technology, too, so he couldn't make any adjustments. He'd look like a vagabond, or poor...

Nobody pays attention to the poor, even on the Newverse planets. Not until they tried to occupy the same space as the wealthy, anyway. This disguise would get him most of the way to where they were going unnoticed. He took off the scrubs top with a hiss of pain. With a guilty flush, he recalled the feel of Meris' hands on his body as she had helped him dress at the hospital.

"Don't be a fool," he told himself, jerking the rough canvas shirt on and buttoning it.

There was no underwear in the boxes, not that he relished the idea of wearing some that didn't belong to him anyway. He hobbled to the bathroom and found a pair of scissors to cut the legs off the scrub pant instead. The trousers fit over his makeshift undergarments with plenty of spare room, but his ankles were left bare. He went back and found a belt and thick wool socks and a tall pair of boots that covered the gap. The woman who had once lived in this cottage had likely been a widow, he surmised, and the fact that all this clothing was still here led him to believe she had probably died herself by now. Still, he felt guilty for taking her husband's clothes.

But not nearly as guilty as he felt for pining for Ellias Gammett's fiancée, even if the man was dead.

"I said, stop being a fool," he chided himself again.

"Talking to yourself now, are you? Careful, people might say you're mad."

He jerked his head toward the doorway. Berent Gaehts stood there, airbolt gun aimed at Darius' chest. Slowly, Darius held his hands up and out, stepping away from the closet. "Berent. Where's Leo?"

"Don't worry; there's a fifty-fifty chance he'll survive. At least for a few hours." There was dried blood running down Berent's right arm, which he held against his stomach, and he held the gun in his left hand.

"What about the others? What have you done?"

"That's all you care about, isn't it? What *I've* done, what *I've* been accused of. You were going to take everything away from me based on *rumors*. On lies and the whispers of jealous men. But not now, huh? Cuz now I'm the one who's taken everything from you."

Darius shook his head. "Not for long. The truth will come out."

The Riekan shrugged his broad shoulders. "Maybe. But you won't be around to see it." He eyed the airbolt gun as if considering whether to use it.

He couldn't fight Berent in his current state, and he certainly couldn't dodge a bullet. He had to keep Berent talking. "Please, just tell me if Meris and the others are all right first."

"*Meris* and the others? *Meris*?" He laughed. "Oh, gods, that's hilarious. You want her, don't you?" He lowered the airbolt gun, letting it hang at his hip from the strap across his chest and laughed again as guilt flushed Darius' cheeks. "You are a fool."

"Perhaps I am a fool. But *you* are a madman and a murderer."

Berent lunged at him, grabbing a fistful of the borrowed shirt and dragged him across the room to slam against the wall next to the door. Darius stifled a yelp of pain but kept his hands up. If he didn't fight back, the enraged Riekan might back down. "My wife is dead because of you," Berent snarled.

The news hit him just as hard as the fists that had beaten him only days prior. Myranda? No, she couldn't be... but why would Berent lie about that? "What – what did you say?"

"Tried to plan an ambush on me, did you? Tried to use my traitorous wife against me. Didn't work. I got to them first, you see. And now she's dead." His eyes filled with tears that coursed down the flat planes of his face. He choked back a sob. "You made me kill her. Just like you made me kill Ellias. *You* did this!"

He's completely insane... Berent slammed him against the wall again and again. His frenzied anger and grief would send him berserk if Darius didn't do something to stop him.

After his back hit the wall a fourth time, Darius grabbed the Riekan's face in both of his hands as he would an upset child. "Berent, listen to me: I am sorry about wanting to fire you. That was wrong of me. You were right, I should not have listened to rumors. I should have talked to you directly."

Tears still poured down the man's face. "You tried to ruin me!" His voice was a hoarse sob.

"I didn't know. I believed the others; I didn't realize that it wasn't the truth." Tears dripped on his fingers and he wiped them on the Riekan's shoulder. "I am sorry, Berent."

He jabbed one of his uninjured fingers into the wound on Berent's arm at the same time as he kneed him in the groin. Berent doubled over, gasping in pain. Darius lurched out of the room, pulling the door shut behind him. He tried to run, but the damage to his body wouldn't allow more than a slow trot. There's no way he could escape Berent. He exited the cottage, looking for something to defend himself with or somewhere he might be able to hide.

Leo. Leo was here somewhere, hurt. Berent had said there was only a fifty-fifty chance of surviving. He had to find Leo, help him if he could, of course, but also to use his vid-phone to warn Meris to stay away from here. If they came back now, Berent would hunt each of them down and kill them as well. He had to live long enough to get a warning to them.

The next cottage was no more than half an acre from the one in which they had been staying, but it felt like a million miles. When he finally reached it, he was panting and sweating. His surgical site had ripped open, too, and a trickle of blood leaked out from under the gel seal. He tried the door handle. It was locked.

An airbolt thudded into the doorframe next to his head, splintering the wood. He scrambled around the side of the cottage, circling toward the back. A small transporter with a tarp thrown halfway off it sat in the back yard. And on the ground next to it –

"Leo!" Darius hobbled to the fallen Sendrassan. Blood pumped from a wound to his abdomen, but he was still conscious, gasping in panicked pain.

"Oh, dear God, help us," Darius begged, kneeling by his comrade. "Leo, can you hear me?"

Leo held up a keycard. "Take it. It runs." He was panting, his face extremely pale.

"I'm not leaving you." But he took the keycard Leo pressed into his hand.

"Behind you," Leo said in a strangled whisper.

Darius lurched sideways as another airbolt whizzed past his head. Reluctant to leave Leo unguarded, but knowing Berent would kill them both if he stayed put, Darius scrambled under the transporter. Berent growled in frustration as he approached the vehicle, stopping next to the wounded Sendrassan. Almost casually, he aimed the airbolt gun at Leo's head and pulled the trigger.

"No!" Alazar stifled his scream of grief and anger and scooted back to put the tarp between himself and the Riekan, peeking through a small hole in the material. Berent knelt and looked under the transporter, but he couldn't see Alazar behind the tarp. He stood and circled the vehicle.

Alazar scrambled back to the other side, momentarily stunned at the sight of Leo's lifeless body. But then he grabbed the vid-phone from Leo's pockets and unlocked the transporter's door with the keycard. He slid into the driver's seat with a grunt of pain, his vision getting swimmy, and used the keycard to power the vehicle up. The transporter lifted a few feet off the ground, the tarp sliding off to land at Berent's feet. The Riekan shot a few 'bolts into the side panel, but

Alazar was able to take to the air, leaving Berent – and Leo – far below.

The tears came then as adrenaline and fear ebbed away to be replaced by grief and shame. And anger. Wiping his eyes, he tapped the vid-phone screen and dialed Meris. She answered almost immediately, her eyes and nose red-rimmed. It must be true; Myranda must really be dead.

"Darius?" she asked, looking at him then over his shoulder before back to him. "What's wrong? What happened?"

"Don't come back to the cottage. Berent found us."

She gasped, new tears springing to her eyes. "Are you all right? Where's Leo?"

He shook his head. "Berent... Leo's gone."

She started crying and he noticed blood in her hair and bruising on her cheek. "Meris, you and the others...?"

"He killed Myranda, too. But Wyll, Zac and I, we're alive. We're almost there, we'll come to you."

"No! You must stay away. I won't let anyone else die for me."

She took Ellias' dog tags between her fingers, caressing them. "You won't survive alone if he catches up with you. Not in your condition."

"Leo was able to get the video out to all social media platforms before – but there was no time for the mainstream. Just see if there is still a way to upload it onto the Nexus mainstream. If not, go to ground. Lay low until all of this is over."

Her brow furrowed. "What are you going to do?"

He swallowed hard. If this was the last time he got to speak to her... "I know I shouldn't say this, but... I... I care for you.

Deeply. I know you can't feel the same way for me, I know that. I just... I needed you to know. In case. Nothing more."

She looked into his eyes a long moment. A tear traced down her cheek. "I know, Darius."

He smiled. "You'll know when it's safe for you again."

He disconnected before she could respond. A still shot of the last moment of the call stayed frozen on the screen a few seconds after, and he ran his thumb down her cheek. Then he tossed the phone out the door hatch and changed course for Bradenbern, New Holland.

He would go into the heart of the Capitol. He would go straight to the Council.

CHAPTER 16 – MERIS

She set the vid-phone down and buried her face in her hands. Just a moment to grieve for Leo, that's all she could give herself now. "Wyll," she said, running her hands up across her hair with a sniff. "Wyll," she repeated, louder.

"What did he say? What happened?"

She got up and knelt between the front two seats where he and Zac sat. "We can't go back to the cottage." She sniffled again. "Berent found it."

Zac groaned and leaned his head against the back of the seat. Wyll closed his eyes briefly before adjusting their course away from the farm, which was now visible on the horizon. "How bad?" he asked.

"Darius made it out, barely." She paused a second, a trembling deep inside her. "But Leo..."

Zac banged his head against the headrest once. "Why does this keep happening?"

Wyll's jaw clenched and unclenched, tears pooling in his eyes. "It was the trackers again. He would have been able to tell everywhere we'd been since the beginning. I bet that's even how he knew to find us in the Security Compound. He wasn't looking for me on the monitors, he was following her. He knew from the beginning she'd betrayed him to us." He slammed his fist on the seat's armrest. "I should have seen this coming."

"What do we do now?" Zac asked. "Where's Alazar going?"

"He didn't say." She thought back on his last words to her, and how they had felt like good-bye. "He only told me he wanted us to go to ground. But if I'm right about where I think he's headed, he's going to need us."

Wyll and Zac exchanged a look, both nodding after a moment's consideration. "Where are we headed, then?"

She shivered, fearing what would come next. "The Council Court."

Four hours later, and only an hour before twilight, they hovered over the rise of a hill to the southwest of Bradenbern. Even from here, they could see clouds of smoke and hear the distant sound of weapons firing. All the chaos seemed focused on an area of the city toward the north.

"Please tell me that's not where the Council Court is," Zac said.

"It is," Meris replied. "But I don't understand. Who would be fighting? You don't think – you don't think they attacked Darius' transporter, do you?" She was trembling inside again.

"There's only one way to find out," Wyll said, taking them across the hill and into the city.

There were fires here and there. The streets were packed with people carrying signs and protesting. Enforcers and what looked like soldiers squared off against the citizens. She couldn't see what the signs said from up here, but the chaos and carnage of the rioting were plain to see.

You started a riot, Miss Brand...

"Are we sure this is a good idea?" Zac asked. "I mean, we don't have any idea what's happening or what will happen to us once we get close."

"We can't just abandon him," Meris said. "We all agreed to this."

"Yes, but that was before we knew the whole city was going up in flames. It's not just the Council and Enforcers we're dealing with now. Those are Federal soldiers down there," he added, pointing out a knot of Wardens fending off a group of protestors.

"We take our chances," Wyll said. "If we don't help Alazar tell the truth, Berent wins." The muscle in his jaw twitched. "And my sister and Leo died for nothing."

Zac nodded and turned his attention back to the scenes below. It was just like Stell-Ore, only on a larger scale. Wyll took them in to approach the Council Court, but before they even got two blocks from it, they were met with a wall of opposition. Dozens of Law Enforcement Vehicles hovered in a protective perimeter encircling the Court, flashing their turquoise and amber lights. The one closest to their transporter bleeped its siren and zoomed forward to intercept them.

Over a loudspeaker, the LEV pilot barked out his commands. "Unidentified transport vessel, touch down and await to be boarded for interrogation and inspection."

"They can't do that," Zac said. "There are protocols, they can't board without permission."

"They can with probable cause or during times of war," Wyll reminded him.

"War?" Meris asked. "Riots, sure, but that's not war down there." She frowned, getting back into her seat and buckling in. "Is it?"

"We'll find out," Wyll said, lowering the transporter onto the nearest flat rooftop and shutting off the ignition. He pressed the button to open the doors and they all waited strapped into their seats for the Enforcers to approach.

The LEV set down in front of them and, after a moment, two Enforcers exited. Meris had never been in trouble with the law and seeing these armed and armored men heading toward them made her nervous. It was like the first time she found herself on the wrong end of Wyll's gun, what seemed like a lifetime ago.

The first Enforcer got to them and warily examined the interior from a few feet away. "State your business here," he ordered Wyll, gun at ready but not actively aimed at him.

"My name is Wyll Meiryg, these are Zac Colphin and Meris Brand. We need to speak to the Council."

The Enforcer made no sound, but the stiffening of his posture told them he knew who they were. His comrade got on his radio to report their identities, while the first Enforcer brought the muzzle of his airbolt gun up to aim at Wyll's chest. But a sudden warning cry from the second Enforcer made him spin toward his right just in time for both of them to be pinned down in a hail of bullets.

"Hold on!" Wyll shouted, turning on the transporter and wheeling it around, trying to place it between the Enforcers and the attackers.

But before he could get into position, a blinding and deafening blast threw the Enforcers back several feet and lifted their transporter to land nose-first with a crushing thud on the roof of the Enforcers' LEV before sliding off with another crashing thud. The transporter was smoking and hissing, fire licking into the compartment from the damaged engines. Meris had managed to buckle her safety harness just as Wyll turned the transporter back on, but she still felt like a rag doll that had been tumbled through a washer-dryer. Again.

"Wyll? Zac?" She coughed on the smoke that was quickly filling the compartment.

Zac groaned, then his head jerked up as a scream of agonizing pain tore from his throat. Wyll came to with a start, his attention immediately turned to his comrade. "Zac? What's wrong?"

"My leg," Zac said through gritted teeth. "Oh, please God, my leg..."

Meris unbuckled and moved forward to help Wyll with Zac. She gasped and nearly fainted when she saw the control console had crushed inward, mangling Zac's right leg between it and his seat. A broken shard of the plastex console stuck through his torn flesh and blood oozed out at an alarming rate. The fire from the engines was fast encroaching. His leg would also be on fire soon if they didn't get him out.

Meris and Wyll worked together to get Zac unbuckled and his seat maneuvered back as far as it could go. With each touch, each movement, he stifled another scream. The pain must be unbearable, and Meris prayed for help for her and Wyll, and relief for Zac. Once the seat was moved back as far as it would go, she and Wyll prepared to try turning the seat to pull his leg further out of the wreckage.

"On three, Meris. One, two, three!" She and Wyll tried swiveling the seat.

"Gahh! Wait! Stop, stop, stop," Zac pleaded, tears coursing down his face. They stopped and he took a deep breath, letting it out slowly and shakily. "It's not going to work."

The smoke was getting worse. They were all coughing now. "We can't leave you in here. This thing's going to go up any minute," Wyll said.

"Where's the extinguisher?" Meris asked, searching the control panel for the right switch.

Wyll tapped a couple of buttons on the control console. A sputtering, weak stream of fire suppressant hissed out of various vents inside the compartment, but it wasn't enough to completely extinguish the fires. Meris looked around in the back of the compartment, and finally found one small back up hand-held extinguisher. This was of the more primitive design that had been used back on earth and she knew the chemicals inside this container would be almost as toxic as the smoke itself. She leaned across Zac and sprayed the extinguisher, trying to block him and her own face from the blowback of the chemical foam.

Finally, the worst of the fire was out, though the smell of smoke and chemicals hung thick in the air. She moved off of Zac as quickly as possible, apologizing for causing him more pain. He gave her a weak smile, panting with the effort of staying conscious.

"S'okay," he said. "You saved me from turning into a crispy critter, so a little extra pain is worth it." He said in his usual flippant way, but she could see the fear and absolute agony he was experiencing reflected in his aqua eyes.

She turned to Wyll. "How are we –"

Another blast nearby sent the transporter skidding sideways a few feet. Seconds later, there was pounding on the hull. "Open up! You have to get out of there!"

Wyll and Meris exchanged a look. She shrugged. There was no way to tell who was who outside, or who posed a threat to them and who didn't. They had to take a chance, however; there was no way they could stay inside the transporter. Wyll growled in frustration and opened the doors again.

Two women, dressed in civilian clothing but carrying M4s, stood just outside. They swept their gazes across the interior of the compartment. "Another bombing is coming," the first woman, a dark-haired middle-aged Riekan, said.

"Our friend," Meris said, pointing to Zac. "His leg is trapped."

She jumped aboard and approached Zac's seat. She swore under her breath when she saw the extent of the damage. Giving him a hard, intense look, she said, "This is going to hurt."

"Excuse me?"

She lifted a plasma knife, similar to the laser saw Wyll had used in his fight against the enraged and super-armored Pentarian back at Stell-Ore. She brought the knife down in one decisive, quick motion. Meris and Wyll yelled and lunged forward as Zac screamed. But the plasma knife bit into the base holding up his chair, sending it toppling off sideways. Zac landed with a yelp. But his leg dropped free of the wrecked dashboard.

Blood spurted from a gash just above his knee now that the twisted metal and plastex was no longer plugging the wound and compressing the artery. Another boom echoed in the distance. "We gotta get him to a doctor," Meris said.

The Riekan shook her head and pulled Zac away from the ruined chair. She knelt next to him and lifted the knife again. "No time. Do not move."

He went still, his eyes locked on hers. After a second's hesitation, he said, "Do it."

She yanked out the plastex shard then brought the knife down carefully until it contacted the wound. The smell of burning flesh filled the cabin. Zac screamed briefly, before passing out.

The woman turned to a stunned Meris and Wyll. "You'll have to carry him out. We'll cover you." Then she jumped back out onto the roof to rejoin her comrade.

Meris shook herself out of her shocked daze and helped Wyll pull the unconscious Zac to his feet. The wound had immediately cauterized, so his leg was not bleeding, but seeing and smelling the burned skin nearly made her throw up. The mysterious woman motioned to them through the open door.

Chaos met their eyes the moment they stepped off the transporter. Civilians and Enforcers clashed hand to hand and transporter to transporter as far as they could see. Smoke filled the air, as did the sounds of gunfire – both of the airbolt and gunpowder-based varieties – and booming bombs. The Riekan woman led them to another transporter hovering above the edge of the building. She waved her hand and the transporter lowered even with the roof ledge, pivoting so its open doors faced them. The other woman, a tall Sindrian, leapt across the narrow strip of empty air onto the transporter. The Riekan covered the three of them as they passed Zac off into the

Sindrian woman's grasp, then as Wyll and Meris made the jump themselves. She then joined them, still firing at the encroaching combatants.

"What is going on out there?" Meris demanded once the doors had shut and the transporter took off.

The Riekan woman looked at her like she was crazy. "You are Meris Brand, are you not?"

"Y-yes," she replied cautiously.

"Then welcome to your war, Miss Brand. I'm Lilla, this is Yerna. We are Wardens of the Council Court." She gave her a half smile and chuckled lightly. "Berent is not going to believe you're here."

CHAPTER 17 – MERIS

"Tell them to stop the transporter, now," Wyll demanded in a deadly quiet voice. He'd sprung across the compartment and had one hand on the Riekan woman's throat, and with his other, he'd taken her gun and pointed it at the Sindrian. Meris still wasn't sure how he'd done it so fast.

The Sindrian, Yerna, had her gun aimed at Wyll, the two locked in a stalemate. But at a gesture from Lilla, she lowered the weapon and held her hands out in a submissive posture. "It's not safe to land here," she said. "But we will touch down soon enough."

"No. You let us out of here, now. I'm not letting you hand us over to Berent Gaehts. I should have known better than to get on board with a Riekan."

Lilla tapped his hand and tried to speak. He relaxed his grip just enough to allow speech, but not to break free. "You misunderstand. I meant that he would not believe you came here. Not after Alazar-"

His grip tightened and her words choked off. "What happened to Alazar?"

"Wyll, for pity's sake, let the woman breathe and talk to us," Meris said, pulling on his arm. "She did save our lives."

He gave her a dark look but released their Riekan rescuer. She massaged her throat and gave Meris a grateful nod. "Alazar arrived in the city half an hour ago. Already, the war in the streets was fully underway, after the video hit the Mainstream."

"How did that happen? Our friend was killed before he could hack the Nexus," Meris said. "He only got as far as uploading it to social media."

The Riekan smiled. "That's all it took. Alazar supporters shared and shared it, and then someone hijacked a newsfeed and broadcast it. The Nexus Mainstream has been playing it on a loop. Commentators have weighed in for and against both sides of the conflict. Survivors from Stell-Ore descended on the Court, some demanding Alazar's name be cleared, some wanting his head on a platter. These protests turned to riots turned to full-on war over the course of a single afternoon as more and more people joined the fray. By the time Alazar had arrived here, the Council was salivating to get their hands on both him and Berent and sort out the truth to avoid any more bloodshed."

"But Alazar's here? He's alive?"

"Yes. He's with the Council."

"Oh, thank you, God," Meris said, her relief overwhelming.

"All of Sindria is waiting with bated breath to see what the Council decides, who they believe. Now that you're here, I think the truth should become quite clear."

"Then you have to get us into the Council Court," Wyll said.

"That's not exactly what I had in mind." She kicked Wyll in the stomach, sending him staggering backward.

"Lilla, what are you-?" The surprised Yerna aimed her gun at the Riekan, but Lilla kicked it from her grasp.

Wyll regained his footing and lifted her gun, but Lilla rushed him, pushing the muzzle toward the ceiling. Meris kicked Yerna's gun back to her and then concentrated on keeping Zac out of the crossfire. Lilla redirected Wyll's hand to aim at Yerna and squeezed the trigger with her finger over his before the Sindrian Warden could fire. The shot rang out deafeningly loud in the small space. Yerna fell back against the side panel with a grunt, blood blossoming on her chest.

"No!" Wyll and Meris both shouted at once.

Zac startled and opened his eyes, but Lilla kicked out one foot, catching him at the temple and knocking him out again. Wyll grabbed Lilla by the throat again and shoved her back, following through to tackle her to the ground. Her head smacked the floor with an audible thwack and Meris thought she'd been knocked unconscious. Meris scrambled over to Yerna.

"Oh, please, God," she prayed, seeing the wound just under the Sindrian woman's collarbone. "Yerna, can you hear me?" She placed the palm of her hand over the bullet hole, trying to stop the bleeding.

The Sindrian Warden's eyes were unfocused, and her breathing was rapid, shallow and making a crackling, burbling sound that froze Meris' blood. Yerna whimpered and grabbed Meris' hand. "Didn't know," she gasped. "Forgive me."

"You're going to be all right," Meris said, hoping it might be true but fearing it wasn't.

Yerna coughed and blood spilled over her lip. "Edzard," she wheezed, "trust only-" a cough wracked her whole body. "Only Edzard." Her pale blue eyes went wide as she desperately tried to breathe but could only choke on the blood that filled her throat. She suddenly went still, her body going slack. Her eyes remained open, staring now at nothing.

Meris fought back tears at yet another life lost and turned around in time to see Lilla had regained the upper hand. She now had sole possession of the gun and was sitting astride Wyll with it pointed at his face. He froze, his hands out in surrender. Meris started to reach for Yerna's gun. Without taking her eyes off Wyll, Lilla said, "Move even an inch, Miss Brand, and you all die, starting with him."

"Don't worry, Meris," Wyll said. "Berent wouldn't like it if she robbed him of the pleasure."

He didn't sound scared, but she knew that he was trained to handle situations like this. She, on the other hand, was trembling with fear. She sucked in a breath and said, "Lilla, please don't."

The Riekan woman smiled at Wyll, then hit him with the butt of the gun, knocking him out. She retrieved restraints from one of the many pockets of her pants and bound his wrists together. When she was done with Wyll, Lilla approached Meris, gun pointed at her. "Hands together," she instructed.

Meris had no choice but to comply. "You killed her," she said.

What looked like regret flashed in the Warden's nut-brown eyes. "She would have killed me if I hadn't." She cinched the thin, adjustable plastex loops around Meris' wrists.

"Because you attacked us. Because you betrayed your duty."

Her eyes burned with anger. "No, I am fulfilling my duty. You three are fugitives, wanted by every law enforcement agency on this planet."

"Then why not take us to the Council Court? Why take us to Berent Gaehts, who is also wanted by every law enforcement agency on this planet. Your duty is to the law, not to a murdering psychopath."

Lilla cocked her hand back as if to backhand her but refrained at the last moment. "Darius Alazar is the murdering psychopath. I don't know how he got to you, twisted your thinking, but he is the real villain here and you of all people should know that."

"He was framed, he didn't kill the crew of Cartage 15. Berent Gaehts and Commander Hauher did. And Berent murdered his own wife, my friend, right in front of me, too. He also murdered Leo Hull and tried to kill Darius Alazar, too. He's insane!"

"You shut your mouth if you don't want me to throw you off this transporter." She turned away and used another set of restraints on Zac, who was still unconscious.

Wyll was starting to come to. Lilla gestured for Meris to move over next to him, positioning herself near Zac, but also where she could keep an eye on the two of them. Wyll groaned and started to put a hand to his face but stopped when he saw the restraints. He twisted around until he saw Meris, and then Lilla. She sat next to Zac's vulnerable body, training the gun on him.

"I don't think either of you are quicker than a bullet, but if you'd like to test my theory, please go right ahead. Berent doesn't care what happens to him, he's only interested in the two of you." She gave them a moment to try something, then almost looked disappointed when they didn't. "Settle in, then. It will be a while before we arrive."

CHAPTER 18 – ALAZAR

A pair of Tudoryan Wardens had taken him directly to the Infirmary the moment his transporter turned up outside the Council Court. A veritable maze of corridors now lay between him and the outside world; there was no going back, for better or worse. The Infirmary, inadequately named, he felt, since it looked like a full hospital only slightly scaled down, was two levels beneath the ground floor and was bright and sterile in that same way that all institutions of health were. The doctor, an older, amiable-looking Sindrian man, gave him a brief examination, patched him up, and announced that he would be fit to give brief testimony, but would require further care immediately after.

They hadn't put him in restraints, which, he decided, was a good sign, but the keen and watchful eyes of the Wardens left him with no doubts that this did not mean he wasn't suspect in their minds. Taking an elevator, they arrived back up on the ground floor. The elevator doors parted, and he was once again surrounded by a corridor made entirely of carraigstone, the pale cream marble-like stone discovered on Tudorya. The name was a point of contention among Earthborns and Earth scholars, as carraig was the Old-Earth Irish word for stone; in essence, they had named it "stone stone." But now, so many years after the settling of the Newverse and the establishment of a new language for each planet plus the interplanetary common tongue that had replaced all previous Earth languages, such squabbles were slowly being forgotten. But the beauty of carraigstone never stops being breathtaking.

No windows let any natural light into this space. It was instead illuminated with a multitude of cut-glass lamps, which threw patterns of light across the vaulted ceiling. It was both calming and slightly disorienting in its beauty.

Further down this hallway, they made a turn to the right, and then almost immediately, another to the left and passed through a set of arched double doors that opened onto a long passage, shaped like the doorway only larger and taller, with floors and columns and supports of the glass walls and ceiling all of carraigstone. Along the middle of the hall were railed-off openings overlooking the floor below, bathing it in natural light as well. He was led past these down one short flight of steps and across the larger intersecting hallway to another short flight of stairs at the far end of the corridor. This led to another intersecting hallway and a collection of tall carraigstone columns that supported the spire overhead. Taking the left-hand corridor, they made their way down another hallway much like the one they had just been in, only wider and intermittently punctuated by tall arched stained-glass windows. From what he could tell, in the brief moments he was able to view them, the windows depicted scenes from the 50-year history of Sindria, the Newverse's youngest colony-planet.

At the end of this corridor, an enormous set of carraigstone doors carved with intricate figures and symbols, much like a tapestry, loomed before them. Six Enforcers stood on each side of the doors, armed and armored to take on an army. The Wardens showed no sign of being intimidated by these officers.

The dark-haired Tudoryan to his right said, "Tell the Council we have located the one they seek. We have Darius Alazar."

The way the Warden spoke his name sent a faint shiver down Darius' spine. It could very well turn out that he'd never leave this place alive. He thought of the last glimpse he'd had of Meris, held onto it like a lifeline that kept him from drowning in anxiety and fear. One of the Enforcers broke formation and slipped through a smaller door set inside the larger ones. He was gone only moments before the large doors slowly swung open. Bright light, warm and pure, spilled into the corridor, dazzling his eyes. It was several seconds before he could see properly again, almost like someone had set off a flash-cap.

The room was huge. High, rib-vaulted ceilings soared into the heavens, with narrow arched windows set high up to allow natural light in. But it was not these windows that caused the dazzling light; a suspended faceted crystal larger than most people's homes concentrated their light and scattered it to every corner and niche in what would otherwise be a cold, dreary stone box. It was as beautiful as it was simple, as magical as it was practical.

All along the two walls to the left and right were tiers of seats, full of spectators, and Darius was reminded of the coliseums of ancient Earth's nearly lost history. The third wall, the one directly ahead of him, held an enormous carraigstone dais with a massive podium that stretched from one end of the dais to the other. Behind this podium were seven throne-like chairs. In each of these chairs was a man or woman, clothed in fine but somewhat plain robes, each a different color: the Council Adjudicators.

He knew that each of these Council members were from one of the seven colony-planets of the Newverse, and their robes indicated which was which. His eyes sought out the ice-blue robes of Sindria and saw a woman of noble bearing wearing them. She was like something out of the ancient Nordic myths from the dying planet left behind.

She stood and held out a hand toward him and the Wardens. "Lead him to the Testimony Box."

There were literal boxes – more like cages, really – one on each side of the area directly before the Council dais, each probably ten feet wide and tall, made of steel bars and sitting atop tall carraigstone plinths. A narrow set of stairs led up to each of them. Standing on each plinth next to each box was a man in a black robe: the Barristers. The Wardens nudged him to start walking toward the base of the steps leading up to the Box on the right. A small Sendrassan man, as short as Meris, scurried toward them from a seat on the lowest tier, carrying a long metal case. He gave it to one Warden to hold, then opened it to reveal several syringes filled with a clear liquid. He took one and approached Darius.

Without thinking, Darius grabbed the man's wrist before the needle came too close.

"Stop," the Sindrian Adjudicator hissed, teeth bared. "If you wish to speak, you will accept the serum. If you'd rather waste the Council's time, you will be held in contempt."

"My apologies, Your Honor. I was not aware of this... custom. What is this serum? What is its purpose?"

She looked startled and somewhat embarrassed. "Forgive us, Darius Alazar. It was our understanding that this procedure was common knowledge."

"Not to me, My Lady."

"It simply ensures you will speak only the truth."

"A truth serum?" he asked, shocked. "Since when has the Council resorted to such barbaric tactics as chemical interrogations? Wasn't that outlawed on Earth?"

"On Earth, yes, Mr. Alazar," the red-robed Riekan Adjudicator, a stout, broad-faced man of middle age, said imperiously. "But we are not on Earth, nor do we hold to Earth laws and customs any longer. The serum has been in use for over a decade and has been instrumental in ensuring justice is served."

"But it was proven unreliable, proven to make some people say whatever was expected of them, whether it was true or not. And the side-effects-"

"Have all been eradicated," the Sindrian Adjudicator assured him. "This serum is the perfected version of Earth's impure, unpredictable counterpart. Have no fear, Mr. Alazar. You will suffer no harm."

He looked the little man in the eye a long moment before releasing his wrist and nodding. The little man tapped the barrel and squeezed a minute portion out of the needle to clear the syringe of any air bubbles, then jabbed it into his arm. The effect of the serum was like the pins-and-needles feeling of a limb gone numb and trying to regain sensation, coupled with a slight burning. He immediately felt like he was in an almost dreamlike state, but this soon faded into a clear-headed though dissociated sharpness. He was alert, but calm and detached. His nervousness and fear were gone.

"Are you ready?" The Adjudicator asked.

"I am."

"Then climb up to the box."

CHAPTER 19 – WYLL

How could he have not seen this coming? He'd allowed himself to be blinded by her status as a Warden, ignoring the fact that she was still just a human – and a Riekan. They may not be as clannish as Tudoryans, but Riekans are loyal to those they consider as their own, often fiercely so. Maybe Lilla was from the same city Berent was, or maybe she even knew him personally. Whatever the reason, she'd allied herself to him, and then used her position to get to him, Zac and Meris before anyone else in the Court could.

"Wardens are supposed to be peacekeepers," Meris said. "What you're doing goes against everything you are supposed to stand for."

"You're wasting your time and breath, Miss Brand," Lilla replied. "Besides, all you're doing is showing your ignorance. Wardens aren't as benevolent as you seem to believe. Do you know why I'm dressed as a civilian? Do you know how many of us there are on the streets at any given moment? Do you know what it is we actually *do* to keep the peace?"

Meris didn't answer, so she continued, "How's your Earth history, Miss Brand? Do you recall agencies such as MI6, CIA, The KGB and the like?"

Meris' face scrunched in confusion. "They were secretive government agencies, shadow organizations. They're rumored to have used less than strictly legal means to gather intelligence and keep tabs on people that may be a threat to their nation's security. Something along those lines."

"Very good. Did you never wonder why there are Law Enforcers and Wardens?"

"I thought Wardens were officers of the Council, separate from Law Enforcement because you serve at a national level, rather than a local level," Wyll said.

"True. But we also operate by much more covert and less than strictly legal means, to borrow her turn of phrase. We get our hands dirty when no one else can or will to ensure the security of Sindria as a whole. I am used to blood on my hands and a little abduction is hardly out of the norm."

"But we are not a threat to Sindrian security," Wyll countered.

She actually laughed. "Did you not see what is happening in this city? Your precious Alazar turned on his own people, butchering them, and now lays the blame at Berent Gaehts' feet. The entire populace is divided, fighting amongst themselves and, in turn, the authorities have had to be dispatched against the people to quash these riots. Meanwhile, Bolidium mining and processing has completely ceased. The man you support has brought this nation's capital – this very planet – to its knees in a matter of days. How are you anything but a threat to Sindrian security?"

Wyll started to protest, but she cut him off. "Enough. We're about to land." She leaned to peer around the partition into the cockpit and said something in Riekan.

Meris turned to him. "Do you know what she's saying?" She kept her voice as quiet as possible.

"She's telling the pilot where to land. She said Berent is waiting for us at the pit."

"What pit?"

He shook his head. "I don't know. But I have a feeling we really don't want to find out."

She sat up a little straighter and peered through the small window in the transporter's door. "I think we are very far away from anyone who could help us."

The transporter was descending. They had to get away before they got to where Berent waited for them. He rotated his hands until they were wrist to wrist, then pulled them in toward his chest as hard and fast as he could, breaking his restraints painfully.

"Then we help ourselves." He lunged at Lilla while she was distracted, driving his fist into her sternum.

She grunted and the gun in her hand went off. The impact of his punch had thrown off her aim, though, and she shot the floor next to the seats on which Zac lay. The wounded man startled awake with a scream of pain as Lilla slammed against his mangled leg. With a groan, he kicked her away with his good leg. "What the frick is happening?"

"She's trying to kill us!" Meris yelled back.

Wyll grabbed Lilla's wrist and brought it down on the edge of the seat as hard as he could. With a sharp scream, she dropped the gun but brought her left palm up to catch him just under the chin. He staggered back a step. She followed this up by jumping to her feet and aiming a kick to his knee, but he jumped back to avoid it. Zac used his good leg to kick her in the back, making her stumble forward.

She drew her plasma knife and turned toward Zac, raising it in a reverse grip. Wyll grabbed her by her shirt and threw her against the side wall panel. She shrieked in frustrated anger and slashed at his arm. He caught her wrist in an overhead grip, but not before the blade bit into the side of his forearm. He screamed and twisted her wrist at an unnatural angle toward her forehead until she dropped the knife.

"The door!"

Meris lurched forward to pull the door release handle. Rushing wind that smelled like wood smoke and was littered with bits of dried grass and dust filled the compartment. They all had to take a moment to shield their eyes from incoming debris.

But before he could throw her out, Lilla wriggled her wrist free and brought her cupped hands up to box his ears. He grunted and dropped to his knees, covering his injured ears, the pain nearly unbearable. He dimly heard Zac shout his name. The next thing he knew, Meris yelled something as a blur of movement caught his peripheral vision. He looked up in time to see Zac and Lilla plunge tangled together out the open door.

"NO!" He sprang up and leaned out the door, gripping the safety handle on the inner panel. Lilla and Zac fell screaming the hundred or more yards into a large tract of trees below. "No," he said again, watching the woods recede in the distance in absolute shock

But there was no time to mourn, he and Meris were still in danger. He ran into the cockpit where the large Riekan man sitting there glanced from the rearview camera feed to him in surprise. His dark eyes were wide and his pale skin white as a sheet.

"What have you done?" he asked in a heavily accented voice.

Wyll answered with an elbow strike to his temple. The large man slumped sideways, and the transporter began to tilt. Wyll pulled the heavy Riekan from the pilot's seat and took his place. Blowing out a breath, he took the controls in hand.

A loud beeping followed by a computerized voice issued a warning in the common language from the cockpit's speakers:

<Warning: Biomarkers not identified. Unauthorized pilot. Manual controls will not be engaged.>

"What?" He tugged on the control stick, but the transporter's trajectory did not change. They were still tilted in the last direction the Riekan had moved the stick. "Please, no," he whispered, punching buttons and flipping switches on the control panel.

The beeping emitted again, followed by the same warning. Wyll growled in frustration. They were descending still, but also in a sort of orbiting pattern, making a large circle in the sky. A new, different warning tone blared out of the speaker. This time, the computerized voice warned:

<Crash imminent. Correct course immediately. Warning: Crash imminent. Correct course immediately.>

Wyll abandoned the pilot seat and grabbed the unconscious Riekan, dragging his left hand to wrap it around the control stick. A small chime emitted from the speakers. This was followed by a greeting:

<Welcome, Pilot Ruslan. Warning: Crash imminent. Correct course immediately.>

Wyll leveled the transporter off and tried to pull them out of the spin, but there was too much resistance. He pulled back on the accelerator to slow the vehicle and they immediately started losing altitude again. "God, please," he said through gritted teeth, hauling on the stick to try to straighten them out.

Another stand of trees loomed up before him in the darkening sky. "Meris, hold on!" His voice ripped from his raw throat in a near-panicked yell. He jerked the control stick up and to the left, further into their already spiraling course instead of trying to pull out of it, hoping- praying- that it would be enough to make them clip the edge of the forest instead of crashing into its heart.

They hit the first branches and he pitched forward against the control panel, losing his grip on the Riekan's hand and the control stick. The transporter began to plummet toward the ground, toward the massive tree trunks. He managed to get the pilot's hand back on the stick and reduced their airspeed even more, almost to the point of cutting off the thrusters completely and tilted the vehicle to the right.

Meris screamed in the back compartment, but he couldn't worry about that. They were about to hit another section of tree limbs and he had to make sure the transporter wouldn't take too much damage. They ended up shearing off the branches with the underside of the vehicle, the metal emitting a terrible screech as the limbs scratched and scraped at it, but they were sent veering away from the trees and out of the spiral.

Wyll tilted the transporter until they were level again and effected a fast but controlled descent the last thousand yards. The landing was still a hard one, gouging the grassy turf for half a mile. When the transporter finally came to a stop, he peeled his grip off the stick, and the Riekan's hand fell with a loud thump on the floor in the sudden quiet. He sat in shocked silence for a full ten seconds, before running shaky hands across his sweat-beaded face.

A laugh of utter disbelief and relief bubbled out of him. But it just as quickly left him when he remembered Meris' scream. He pushed himself to his feet, his legs like jelly, and ducked through into the passenger compartment.

Meris was huddled in the back right corner, between the last seat and sidewall panel. Her knees were drawn up to her chin, her arms wrapped around her head. "Meris?"

Slowly, she lifted her head and lowered her arms enough to look at him. "Did we die?"

He chuckled and knelt next her. "Not yet, but if we were anywhere near where Berent was waiting, there's no way he didn't see or hear that landing. We've got to get out of here."

"Will this thing get back up in the air?"

"I don't think so. Besides, it only works with the Riekan pilot's hand, so unless you wanna cut it off and leave him here one-handed, we'll need to hike our way out." He looked around the compartment. "Speaking of cutting, we need to get your restraints off."

Meris sniffed and reached into the small space between her hip and the sidewall panel to pull out the Riekan Warden's plasma knife. "She tried to retrieve this just after she boxed your ears. That's why Zac- why he-" her words dissolved into tears. "He's really gone, isn't he?"

He nodded, then looked at the floor, trying to block the image of Zac falling to the earth from his mind. "There would be no way to survive a fall like that." He took the knife and cut the restraints from her wrists.

"Wyll, your ears are bleeding."

He touched his fingertips to his ears and felt a warm fluid trickling out of them. When he looked at his fingers, they were wet with a red-tinged liquid. "Ruptured eardrums," he told her. "I'll be fine. Come on, we have to get out of here before the pilot wakes up."

CHAPTER 20 – WYLL

Wyll turned off the plasma knife, the arcs of energy winking out, and slid it into his pocket, then helped Meris to her feet. They exited the transporter on shaky legs and found themselves in a vast area of untouched wilderness. Tall, summer-gold grass waved in the stiff breeze all around, blanketing the hilly terrain for miles, punctuated sporadically by tracts of forest. The nearest woods half a mile northwest held the trees their transporter clipped on its violent descent. The next one a mile to the west of that... was where Zac now lay.

"We should take cover in the woods," he told her, "just in case Berent does a flyover trying to spot us."

"What about Yerna? She might have a family. Berent won't take her body back to the city."

"There's nothing we can do for her now. I'm sorry. When this is all over, we can tell someone where to find her."

She nodded and fell into step with him without a word as he trudged toward the closest stand of trees. He estimated they had about fifteen minutes until dusk. He didn't want to get stuck anywhere near Berent once darkness fell. They entered the tree line, staying close enough to the edge to not lose their way, but far enough in to minimize the chance that they might be seen. It was cool and shadowy in the woods. Under other circumstances, he would enjoy the time out in the wild. But right now, he was wrecked, emotionally and physically, and in serious need of food and a shower.

Not more than five minutes into their hike, a Darter – the small personal transport craft modeled after Earth's helicopters – zoomed into view and hovered over the crash site.

"Get down," Wyll warned, slinking further into the trees' shadows. "Och, I was hoping to be further away than this when he showed up."

"He's setting down," Meris said, fear in her voice. "Come on, let's get out of here. He's sure to know we came this way."

She was right. There was no other logical place for them to have gone. He led the way cutting at an angle through the trees, heading toward the northwestern edge of the woods. They would have to pass from this forest into the next one if they hoped to keep Berent from finding them. What they would do after that, he wasn't sure about yet. Near as he could tell, they were between five and ten miles southeast of the city. There was no way they could walk that far in the dark and any light they used from their vid-phones would only serve as a beacon for Berent.

The ground underfoot was soft and slightly damp, as if it had recently rained, but the terrain was uneven and brambly bushes and tufts of tough, long grass entangled their feet as they pressed on. A breeze whiffled through the leaves of the trees and teased their hair in different directions, carrying the green scent of fresh earth and vegetation. They lost sight of the sky, except for small slivers between the crowns of trees. The sound of the Darter's engines fell away to be replaced by the scurryings of small animals and insects, and the occasional birdsong.

Another half an hour passed, and they were at the edge of the woods in the twilight. An open space of roughly a quarter mile lay between their position and the second forest. "We'll need to cover the distance as quickly as possible," he told her. "Are you up for a quick march?"

"I can run that far, no problem. You don't have to go slow for me."

"No, we don't want to run. Not until we have to. We don't have any water or food, or the means to get either at the moment, so we need to conserve as much energy as possible. I'm about at the end of my reserves already, after that fight and bringing that transporter down."

"All right. You set the pace."

He nodded and stepped out of the woods and onto the open, grassy land. He eased into a quick march, tapping the 116 beats-per-minute tempo on his thigh, but cut the pace from 30 inches to 24 to not overexert himself. Though Meris was much shorter, he noticed she had a fairly long pace length and was keeping up well. About halfway across the opening, they heard the engines of the Darter once again approaching.

"Wyll?"

There was nothing to take cover under or behind. He cursed under his breath. "Go! Run!"

She shot ahead of him, sprinting full out. He switched over into a run, as well, and caught up with her. Only a few dozen yards now lay between them and the trees, but the Darter suddenly flew into view, just to their left. Berent leaned out the side window, a HEL-gun in his hand.

"Hurry!" Wyll shouted, grabbing her hand and hauling her toward the trees.

The high-energy laser cut a swath of destruction in the grass not more than two feet from them. A few seconds more and they were finally at the edge of the tree line. This section was much thornier and more filled with tangled underbrush. They went crashing through, startling a large rodent and sending up a frightened flock of birds. The Darter was circling overhead, trying to get a clear shot at them. Wyll cut deeper and deeper into the heart of the forest, angling to the north and west.

Meris stopped dead in her tracks. Wyll stumbled a step beyond her before stopping and turning back. "What? What is it?"

She sniffed the air. "I smell smoke."

Just like in the transporter when they opened the door. He sniffed, too. Wood smoke, like a campfire – or, rather, a bonfire. "We can't stop here, though. We just need to keep going and steer clear of wherever that smoke is coming from."

"I think I know where we are," she said, turning a pale face and large, frightened eyes toward him. "Six miles southeast of Bradenbern are The Gold Forests. The Gold Forests are also home to Forest Canyon."

"Ah. Canyon, not pit," Wyll said, realizing his translation mistake. But something about her expression made him pause. "What is it?"

"Forest Canyon is impossible to get into or out of without highly sophisticated climbing gear. And even then, it's still extremely dangerous to navigate. It's been closed off to the public because so many people have died. All Berent would have to do is get us down there and leave – or kill us and throw us in – and no one would ever find our bodies."

"All the more reason to make sure he doesn't catch up with us."

She still looked frightened but started walking again. The smell of smoke was getting stronger and then, to their right, he caught a glimpse of firelight in the distance. It was hard to tell how far they were from the fire, but his instincts told him they were too close.

He motioned toward the light and then lay his finger across his lips. Meris nodded and followed him silently as they veered more to their left. A sharp twig snap startled him into a crouch, frozen in place, eyes and ears straining for the source of the danger, but his ruptured eardrums were making it difficult to hear clearly.

A rustling from behind. He turned but saw nothing. A quiet, hollow knocking sound, this time from back the other way, ahead and to his right.

Meris put her hand on his arm, squeezing it tight. He could feel her trembling. They both were searching the thick brambles and dense trees for any sign of an enemy. He drew the plasma knife and flicked it on.

There was no birdsong, even the insects had stopped chirping. He eased his left hand down to close on a large rock. It was no airbolt gun or M4, but it could still be lethal long-range if used correctly. He knew how to use it correctly.

He heard Meris' sharp intake of breath a fraction of a second before the thrashing of underbrush as someone rushed them. He had only a moment to register that the man aiming a wooden staff at his face was not Berent before twisting to the side and taking the hit on his right shoulder instead. Pain blossomed across his chest and down his arm, the momentum of the strike knocking the knife from his hand and staggering him down onto his backside.

The man followed through with another strike aimed at Wyll's chest, only this time with the sharp spearhead end of the staff. Wyll rolled to his left and the spear sunk into the soft earth, scoring a gash across his back on its way down. He yelled, then grabbed the staff with his right arm and jerked it side to side to try to make the man loosen his grip. When that didn't work, Wyll brought the rock up to smash one of the man's hands. Bones snapped with an audible crunch.

With an enraged howl, the attacker let go of the staff and cradled his broken hand to his chest. Wyll had a moment then to notice that he was a Pentarian, tall and grey-skinned, as all Pentarians were. Wyll pulled the spear out of the ground to try to run him through, but the man deflected it and knocked the staff from his hands. His kick caught Wyll in the chest, knocking the air from his lungs painfully. Wyll scooted back a few feet to regain his breath and rethink his strategy.

But then, with a raw roar, Meris heaved a large rock at the Pentarian's chest. He flinched away, but it still struck him a glancing blow. He turned toward her. She cast about for another weapon but had nothing in hand. The big man backhanded her to the ground.

"Hey!"

Wyll gathered himself up and sprang at the Pentarian before he could advance on her again. He tackled the man, the two of them crashing to the ground in a painful tangle of limbs. Wyll maneuvered around to maintain the upper hand.

He was breathing hard, on the verge of collapse, but couldn't rest even a moment. He swung his fist at the bigger man's face, the blow connecting with a jarring impact. He pulled his arm back for another strike, but the Pentarian caught his fist in one hand and heaved his hips and legs to toss Wyll off. Wyll's back struck a log as he landed, knocking the wind out of him again. Pain made his head muzzy, exhaustion made him slow.

The Pentarian man stood and stomped toward him and Wyll knew in that moment that he could not win this fight. Either this man was going to kill him here in the woods, or he was going to take him to Berent. Either way ended in death. His heart pounded and his hands trembled, and yet a calm was settling over him as well. At least he would be with Myranda and those who'd gone before soon.

But if he died, that would leave Meris in danger. No, he had to keep fighting as long as possible. Shaking from the effort, Wyll used the log as support and tried to rise to his feet. Before he could straighten all the way up, the Pentarian grabbed him by fistfuls of his shirt and hauled him two feet off the ground. His legs still tingled a bit from the blow to the back, but he managed to kick his attacker in the chest. He was rewarded with a pained grunt. The Pentarian threw him to the ground like a broken doll. Wyll's forehead struck the log and his vision went dark briefly.

He tried once again to lever himself up, to face the end head-on like a soldier, but he was shaking from exhaustion and his various wounds. Instead, he rolled onto his side and watched the Pentarian approach. The man's expression was dispassionate. This was a job, an order to carry out, nothing personal. Wyll had a flash of memory: pulling the trigger of his airbolt rifle, sending the 'bolt through Ellias Gammett's brain, and being similarly unaffected. In the moment, anyway.

He preferred the symmetry of dying the same way than at Berent's hands. Especially since it would rob that maniac of the pleasure.

"Meris, run."

He heaved himself over into a somewhat seated position. The Pentarian smiled and swung the staff over his head until the spear-end pointed at Wyll's chest. Wyll held out both hands, making a beckoning gesture.

"Come on, you ugly mug," he said, spitting toward the man's feet. "Let's see if you've got what it takes."

The Pentarian's expression hardened. He lifted the spear staff for the killing stroke. Just like Wyll intended. *Please, forgive me my many sins, O Lord, and welcome me into Your Kingdom...*

The man's expression seemed to freeze, a short grunt escaping his lips. His grip went slack and the spear staff fell to the ground, disappearing beneath the ferns and grasses of the underbrush. He fell in a boneless heap with a loud whump.

Meris stood behind him, panting. Tears streaked down her face and she was trembling, pale as a carraigstone statue. She stared at the apparently dead Pentarian, eyes wide. A large gash bisected her right eyebrow and blood trickled down her face.

"Meris?"

With a whooshing breath, she doubled over, pressing her hands to her thighs. He thought she was going to either throw up or pass out. But, after a moment, she ran the back on her hand under her nose and shifted her gaze to look at him.

Plucking the plasma knife from where it now stuck out of the back of the Pentarian's neck just below the base of the skull, she turned it off and handed it back to Wyll.

"Please, don't ever drop this again."

He took it and slid it into his pocket. "I promise."

After that, she did throw up.

CHAPTER 21 – ALAZAR

He wasn't sure if it had gone well or not. The Barrister asked him relentless questions, each time seemingly dissatisfied with his answers. The Council sat silently, their expressions unreadable. But toward the end, he felt a subtle shift in the tension of the room, mostly coming from the tiers of spectators rather than the Council or Barrister.

It happened right after the Barrister had been grilling him especially hard, going over the same questions again and again, each time phrased a little differently. After having him yet again confirm that Berent Gaehts and Commander Hauher were the ones really behind the riots at Stell-Ore and the demonstrations and warring in the streets outside the court, Alazar was starting to get tired of hearing the man's pompous voice.

"Yes," he confirmed again. "That is correct. Just as I've said half a dozen times already."

The Barrister laughed unexpectedly. "Forgive me if I find this all a little hard to believe, Mr. Alazar. This seems an awfully complicated and far-fetched way of effecting a hostile corporate takeover."

"You know I'm telling the truth. Berent Gaehts is insane. He nearly choked one of his crewmembers to death on the way home from Nevzaris because the man accidentally took a drink from Berent's canteen instead of his own. Berent thought he was trying to infect him and the crew with some off-world pathogen. Nonsense, of course, and he gave some sort of half-hearted apology, but the crew were afraid of him from then on out."

He looked up at the Adjudicators. "He's been acting impulsively, irrationally. I believe he is making it up as he goes along, and I have no idea what he will do next. That's another reason I sent Meris and the others away: I want them to be as far away from Berent as possible until he is incarcerated"

"Do you have any evidence at all to support your side of the story, Mr. Alazar?" The Barrister asked.

He opened his mouth to speak but paused. "Isn't that what your serum is for?"

The Barrister gave him a smarmy smile. "Actual evidence is still preferred over testimony. What you say under the influence of the serum can only be categorized as what you believe to be true without any proof to back up your claims."

"Then why bother with the serum at all? Not taking the witness' testimony at face value and as fact while the serum is active in their system negates the purpose of using it at all, does it not?"

Someone in the tiers snickered audibly before being shushed. The Barrister's smug expression faltered slightly, but he waved a dismissive hand. "You did not answer the question: do you have any proof?"

"Myranda did. She had stumbled across a recorded conversation between Berent and Hauher when she borrowed her husband's vid-phone a few days after the crew of Cartage 15 were murdered. The conversation was dated the week before the incident and was of the two men discussing using Wyll Meiryg to carry out the order. Hauher thought Wyll would be easy to control because of his tie to Myranda and Berent."

He allowed himself a smile at just how wrong they had been about that. "She copied it and sent it to her tablet, where she also composed an affidavit detailing other things Berent said or did in the days before which had struck her as odd. She went to Stell-Ore to tell her brother. But by then, it was too late. Berent had already started his uprising. Both files are still on her tablet."

He closed his eyes at his own stupidity, and against a wave of lightheadedness. "Which is with Meris and Wyll and Zac."

"Ah," the Barrister said. "Perhaps it was not such a good idea to tell them to go to ground after all."

"It would seem not." He ran a hand across his brow.

A murmur rippled through the crowd of spectators. The Sindrian Adjudicator struck a small gavel on the podium and held up her hand for quiet. "I believe we will pause here, gentlemen. Mr. Alazar needs further medical attention and I do not intend to deprive him of it any longer. Agreed?"

The other Adjudicators each nodded and struck their own gavels. "We are adjourned until tomorrow morning, then."

The Wardens had opened the Box's door and let him out. They assisted him back down the stairs and swiped a keycard to exit through a door set in the wall beside the tiers of spectator seating. They crossed a short hall with a door in each wall and, with another keycard swipe, passed through the door exactly opposite the one by which they had just entered. A comfortably appointed anteroom, much like a home's parlor, now stood before him. Plush settees lined the walls to his right and left, a low wooden table stood next to the one on the right. A bowl of fruit sat on top of it. His stomach had rumbled at the reminder that he had not eaten in an exceedingly long time.

The Warden to his right, the tall, dark red-haired Tudoryan man had assured him he would be fed after he'd been seen by the doctor again. He swiped them out of this anteroom via a door opposite, which turned out to lead down another long, door-lined stone corridor and to an elevator, which they boarded.

A few moments later, the elevator doors had slid open to reveal the Infirmary's waiting room/nurses' station once more. He peered across the gleaming, sterile white room to see the doorway by which he'd been brought here earlier. As before, nurses and other staff passed busily through the area.

He'd been taken to the same exam room as before, and seen to by the same, amiable doctor and medical assistant as before. They'd used a handheld imaging device to determine that he had developed a new, small bleed internally and would need to undergo another, though minor, surgery to repair it. He was now dressed in the eternally unflattering gown every person who has ever had the dubious privilege of being admitted to a hospital has had to endure, and was seated on the exam bed waiting for someone to take him to the OR.

Just then, the amiable doctor's assistant- a rather stiff and slightly unpleasant Sindrian man, returned. He entered the exam room, shoving the privacy curtain to the side with a loud rattle of its hangers. "Right. Now, then, Mr. Alazar, let's get you down to the OR."

He handed Darius a small paper cup with pills inside and another paper cup of water. He looked from the cups to the assistant. "What are these?"

"These are to get a jumpstart on getting you sedated. The anesthesia works better if you're already relaxed. Don't worry," he added quickly at the sight of the frown on Darius' face, "you will still be conscious. Just... relaxed."

He rattled the cup of pills. Darius hesitated just a moment longer before taking it. He peered at the little pills, then swallowed them down with the water. The assistant smiled and gestured for him to lie back on the exam bed. As he lay down, he could almost already feel a difference in the tension of his muscles.

Moments later, feeling every muscle in his body completely at ease for the first time in... years, probably, he was being wheeled to the OR. A mask was placed over his nose and mouth once they arrived, and a voice told him to count backwards from ten. A strange smelling gas filled his lungs as he took a breath to speak.

"Ten, nine... eight... sev-"

CHAPTER 22 – MERIS

Full dark had set in. They crept through the deeper darkness of the forest inch by inch, more by feel than by sight. She had killed a man. The phrase didn't quite capture the reality of the situation. It wasn't just her fault that a man had died, like with all the others. No, she had taken a life. With her own hands.

Please forgive me, Lord. You know I didn't want to do that. But I didn't see any other way to save Wyll. I'm sorry – I should have tried to find another way. I should have trusted You to save him. Please forgive me. Please –

His body had stiffened just a moment before it all went slack. She'd tried to do it as quickly and painlessly as possible, but for the briefest of moments, had he known she'd killed him? Did he have time to feel it? To be afraid?

Just keep walking. Just stay with Wyll. Don't think about it. Don't think about how the plasma blade had sunk into –

STOP! She begged for the memory to stop playing in her mind on a loop. She begged her hand to stop feeling the slight pop as the knife penetrated the Pentarian's vertebra and brain stem. Unable to hold it back any longer, she pressed her left hand – the one not tainted by death – against her mouth and cried.

A hand touched her shoulder and she nearly screamed. But it was just Wyll, groping in the dark to find her. He drew closer and put his arms around her for a moment. She leaned against him as the tears poured from her like hot venom.

"I'm sorry," he whispered after a few seconds, "but we can't stay here. We have to keep going, all right?"

She nodded, sniffling, then wiped her hands across her face. "All right," she murmured.

He squeezed her shoulders and said, "You saved my life back there. Again. I don't know how to make it up to you, especially with what you had-"

A lumbering crashing noise as someone or something moved through the underbrush ahead and to their left interrupted him. Wyll nudged her behind him and drew the plasma knife. "Another of Berent's men?" he asked, barely audible. He didn't flick on the knife until the noise drew closer, but when he did, the dim blue-white light dazzled her eyes in the murk.

The noise stopped approaching, going silent. Wyll used the knife to try to illuminate their surroundings, turning in a tight semi-circle. A few seconds passed before Meris spotted a shadowy figure rise in front of them.

"Wyll," she murmured, tapping his arm and steering him toward the figure.

"Wyll?" A quiet voice issued from the figure. "Meris?"

She knew that voice. Impossible... "Zac?"

The noise of his movements drew closer again, until the plasma knife's light illuminated his face. It looked like Zac. It sounded like Zac. But how could that be?

"Thank God," he said, dropping to his hands and knees in the tangled underbrush.

Meris rushed from Wyll's side and knelt next to the man, still not entirely certain it was who she thought it was. But, sure enough, when she touched a hand to his face and turned it toward her, familiar eyes met hers. "How..."

Zac pulled her into a crushing embrace. "I never thought I'd find you," he said, his voice sounding hollow and haunted.

The light from the knife grew brighter as Wyll approached them. "How is this possible? You- you fell through the sky..."

Zac released her and sat back, running a shaky hand across his face. "Lilla...she hit the trees first. She's dead," he added quickly. "Impaled. I, I don't know how, but I managed to grab hold of her legs. I hit a tree limb, hard, but I didn't let go. I climbed down and, after a while, started off in the direction I last saw you heading."

"A miracle," Meris said, still unsure this was really happening.

Wyll came a little bit closer and reached a hand toward Zac. The moment he made contact with Zac's shoulder, he let out a breath, saying, "Thank you, Lord." He then pulled Zac to his feet, looking him over. "How badly are you hurt? How's your leg? Is that fresh blood?"

Zac chuckled quietly and waved Wyll's hands away. "I'll survive, provided we get back to the city soon. The cauterizing held, but my leg is still mangled up." He hoisted a thick branch. "I've been using this to get this far. What about you two? How did you get away?"

"Long story," Wyll said. "Or at least too long to safely tell here. Berent's on the hunt, we need to get back to the city or find somewhere to hole up until morning."

"As much as I want to get to the Council and Alazar as quickly as possible," Meris said, "I doubt we can get very far in the dark and with Zac's leg as is. My vote is for hiding and waiting out the night."

"Alazar made it to the Council, then?"

"That's right, you were unconscious when they told us that," Meris said. "Yes, he's fine."

"If we can trust anything that Riekan said."

"I don't see how lying about that benefitted her."

Wyll grunted, scoffing, but merely said, "Let's get moving."

Some two hours later, near as she could tell, the wind picked up. Overhead, branches of the towering spruces and pines swayed, emitting unnerving screeches and groans as they flexed and rubbed together. The scent of wood smoke had been left far behind now, replaced by the greener, earthy smells of the deep forest. Every so often, they startled some woodland creature into scurrying away. Each time, Meris' heart did somersaults against her ribcage, convinced it would be Berent charging at them instead.

Zac was fading fast. They all were. But they all also wanted to get as far away as possible before halting for some rest. Wyll had turned off the plasma knife as soon as they had reunited with Zac, and only slivers of moonlight penetrated the thick canopy. Meris could see, but only in differing shades of darkness.

The dense trees abruptly ended, and they found themselves in a clearing. Ferns and shrubs covered the whole area, which was at least twenty or thirty feet across, and the moonlight here was bright enough to identify individual plants. "Thank you, Lord," she said, spying a blackberry bush.

The thorns scratched her fingers and backs of her hands, but she didn't care. Plucking a handful of berries, she passed them to Zac. Wyll helped her pull off another couple of handfuls for the two of them to share. She spotted a cloudberry bush further into the clearing and added a large handful of the tart yellow berries to their feast. Wyll, meanwhile, was searching under the taller vegetation.

She handed him a cloudberry. "What are you looking for?" She dared only a whisper, unsure how close Berent might be.

"Wood sorrel," he said. "Sometimes called sour grass." Then he made a small triumphant noise and lifted a scraggly bit of weeds toward her. He pulled off a few clover-like leaves and chewed them. "Here, all of it's edible." He broke a bulb-like root in half and handed it with its attached leaves to her. "No water to clean it with, but I think a little dirt is the least of our worries right now."

"Thank you," she said, taking the plant. The leaves had a bright and sour taste, a little lemony, and helped quench her thirst almost completely. The bulbous roots looked like misshapen pale carrots, but, surprisingly, tasted a little bit like a potato or turnip. And dirt.

Zac smiled and shoved a large bunch of it into his mouth. "Not exactly a feast, but you know what they say about beggars and choosers and all that."

Meris sank to sit on the damp, cool ground. A moment later, Zac sat next to her. He bumped his shoulder against hers. "Are you all right?" His voice was quiet in the gloom. "I mean, I know we're being quiet cuz Gaehts is hunting us, but you feel off to me."

The tears came, hot and fast, before she could stop them. "Nothing about any of this is all right, Zac. I never meant for any of it. I never meant for anyone to die, and now-" She broke off in a sob, and quickly covered her mouth to stifle the sound.

He put his arm around her and pulled her close. "I know. But I keep trying to tell you that it's Berent's fault, not yours. Berent and Hauher started all of this. But I tell you what - we're going to finish it."

"I killed someone," she whispered, nearly choking on her sobs. "I don't even know his name, or if he had a family, or anyone who loved him, or-" She sobbed again.

Zac shifted and looked her in the eye. "Stop." His voice was quiet, but it hit her like a slap. It wasn't unkind, but it brooked no argument. "You can't do that. Okay? Stop thinking about that. When this is over, you can drive yourself mad with guilt all you want, but now, we all have to focus on surviving. And if you don't want to endanger all our lives, you'll put it out of your mind right now. You have to."

He sounded so much more like Wyll in that moment, she looked at him again to make sure it really was Zac speaking. But then he gave her a sad smile and shrugged. "Trust me, I know what you're feeling. But I also know how dangerous giving into guilt and grief is in the middle of a mission."

She thought then about how he'd drawn his gun on Myranda and Wyll when Jenna had died. How his feeling of responsibility for her had made him react aggressively, putting everyone in danger. That had only been a few days ago. It didn't even seem possible that they hadn't even known each other a full week yet when so much had changed for each of them.

"How do I do that, Zac? I can't stop thinking about it."

"I... I don't know, actually. You just kinda have to focus on the here and now. Don't think too far ahead, don't think back at all. Just survive. For now. I don't have a clue what's going to happen once this is all over."

"I'll go to prison. Then the Chamber. That's what will happen to me after all of this. Maybe all of us."

Zac was silent a long moment. "Then let's make the best of the time we have and bring Berent down with us." He looked at her. "For the ones we've lost."

CHAPTER 23 – WYLL

They rested a while in the clearing. Zac and Meris dozed, lying out of sight on the mossy ground with ferns and other plants rising over them. Wyll took up a position with his back against a broad tree and kept watch, allowing his body to rest while keeping his mind alert. He could feel Berent searching for them, and several times thought he saw movement in the dark shadows of the forest. He kept as still as possible, his hand gripping the plasma knife at the ready. But when two hours passed without incident, he began to wonder if Berent had given up for the night.

He woke the others up and they ate another handful of berries before moving on through the woods and toward civilization. He and Meris had to support Zac between them before long; his mangled leg was getting worse. This made their progress slow and much louder than he would have liked, but there was no other way, short of leaving Zac and sending someone from the Council back for him in a PTV. But after Lilla, he didn't trust anyone but the two people by his side right that moment.

As they neared the final edge of the forest, nearly another two hours later, lights sweeping by overhead made them all freeze. "Berent?" Meris asked in hushed tones.

"The lights are set too wide to be the Darter. Looks more like a LEV or PTV."

"Which could either mean rescue or more danger," Zac muttered.

"I'm going to assume the latter and pray for the former," Wyll said with a scoffing grunt.

"What do we do?" Meris' voice sounded more weary than scared. "If we stay here, we give Berent a chance to catch up to us. If we step out there and they're on his side, they could cut us down where we stand. Either way we risk death. But only one way could result in us being saved."

Wyll sighed. He, too, was far more weary than afraid. "I'll go. I'll draw their attention, and if they kill me, run as far and as fast as you can away from the lights. If they don't, then you can step out and we'll all get picked up and taken to safety."

"Sounds like a good plan," Zac said, "with one tiny major flaw."

"Which is?"

"I can't run. So, if anyone is going out there to be the tethered goat, it's gonna be me."

"No," Meris said forcefully. "I won't let anyone else die for the war I started. Wyll, you can get Zac out of here better than I ever could. If they capture me instead of killing me, then I trust the two of you to find a way to rescue me. If they kill me, at least you two can escape alive."

Wyll smiled grimly. "Here we've been fighting to survive all this time and now we're arguing over who gets to potentially die first. Myranda would be laughing." His voice choked off and died in his throat. What he wouldn't give to hear his sister's laugh one more time.

"We could go together," Zac said. "Chances are we could scatter and they wouldn't be able to hit us all if they start shooting. If they do, then we get to be all poetically heroic and fall as one, as they say."

"But what about Alazar? If we all die, there's no one to help him. Berent wins."

Wyll looked at her. "Alazar's with the Council. We have to believe that'll be enough."

"If we believed that were true, we wouldn't be risking our lives to get to him."

"Yes, but-"

Meris ran for the meadow beyond the trees before he could finish his sentence. She ran to where the nearest light was searching the ground and stood in the beam, shouting and waving her arms. The vehicle's other light swung around to focus on her, too. Wyll's breath caught in his chest as he watched, horrified that he was about to witness her murder but too stunned to look away.

The vehicle began to descend. A man's voice spoke to her over an external speaker. "This is Warden Edzard Kier of the Council. Keep your hands in the air and identify yourself."

Meris lifted her hands and grinned. "Warden Edzard Kier, my name is Meris Brand and I cannot tell you how happy I am to see you."

He was silent a moment, no doubt thrown off by her greeting, then said, "Miss Brand, are you alone?"

Involuntarily, she threw a look toward where he and Zac stood watching. One of Edzard's lights panned toward them, nearly blinding him. He threw up a hand to shield his eyes.

"Step out of the tree line and approach with your hands up."

He and Zac exchanged a look. Meris seemed to trust this guy for some reason, so maybe they could, too. Zac shrugged. Wyll pocketed the plasma knife, raised his hands and stepped out of the trees. "All right, I'm stepping out. But my friend here is injured and I need to help him walk. Will you allow this?"

"I allow it. Move slowly toward the PTV."

Wyll stepped back and threw Zac's arm over his shoulder again. Slowly, the two exited the cover of the trees and joined Meris where she stood. Together, the three of them approached the PTV cautiously. The side door slid open as the PTV touched down. A second Warden, a dark haired Tudoryan man, helped Zac into the vehicle. Just as Wyll stepped back to let Meris enter, a small, bright light stabbed out of the night sky at them.

A HEL-gun beam blasted the ground at Wyll's feet, missing him by a hair's breadth. He stumbled backward. "It's Berent!"

Meris leapt onto the PTV, falling against the Tudoryan Warden. Edzard swiveled the PTV's guns and opened fire on the Darter. Wyll narrowly avoided being gored by the next HEL-gun blast, taking it across his already scored back instead.

Absolute agony like he'd never felt before erupted and engulfed him. Screaming, he pitched forward into the PTV. The Tudoryan Warden hauled him the rest of the way in and slammed the door shut.

Edzard and the Tudoryan Warden were shouting information back and forth to each other, and Meris and Zac were at Wyll's side. But he could only exist in the pain. Fire-like and unending, the pain of the wound angled in a swath across his entire back, obliterating the comparatively minor annoyance of the spear cut. He knew he was lying on his stomach on the floor of the PTV, but he could take in nothing else of his surroundings.

If they were attacked again now, he'd never even see it coming. But if it put an end to this pain, he almost welcomed it.

"It's superficial," someone said. The Tudoryan? "It isn't life-threatening, other than the shock of the pain. How in the worlds did he get hold of a HEL-gun?"

"One of his supporters had a knife designed to break off into the wound, too." Meris. He knew her voice. "If Wyll hadn't been wearing his body armor, it probably would have killed him. Berent has been trying to kill all of us since this began. He did kill Leo Hull and his own wife, Myranda Gaehts."

"We were there." This was Zac. "For Myranda's murder. We witnessed it. And Alazar witnessed Leo's. But that's only part of the reason he's trying to kill us."

There was a booming sound and the floor lurched underneath him. His cries had died down to an agonized whimper, but this jarring motion coaxed another scream from between his gritted teeth. He heard someone shout, "Hold on!"

The PTV lurched to one side and he would have gone sliding across the floor if it hadn't been for the hands stabilizing him. A moment later, something cool settled over the HEL-gun wound, at once sparking new pain and providing some relief. The momentary sting dulled, along with the fierier pain. Soon, he lay panting, numbness spreading across his body.

"Rest now, Lieutenant." The Tudoryan Warden placed a hand on his shoulder. "You are safe."

To verify, Wyll reached for his companions. "Meris... Zac..."

"We're right here, Wyll," Zac assured him. "Berent attacked us but has fallen back. We're safe."

"For now," Meris muttered.

CHAPTER 24 – ALAZAR

Everything was hazy, his mind still fuzzy, but already he could tell that his body was in a much better condition than it had been when he arrived. Or maybe that was just the pain medication. Either way, it was the first time since Berent and Hauher attacked and threw him into The Hole that he was pain-free. He wanted to drift away on the euphoria painlessness brought, but the reality of his situation inserted itself into his awareness.

With a massive effort, he opened his eyes.

A man was watching him. Darius drew back, startled, then noticed his white lab coat. The man, a Riekan with a friendly expression, gave him a small smile. "Apologies, Mister Alazar. I just came to see if you needed anything."

"Ah." He scrunched his brows together. "Actually, I don't quite know yet. I think I'm all right."

"How is your pain?"

He took a moment to really assess his condition. "I... I don't feel any pain at the moment." He smiled. "For the first time in days, I don't hurt anywhere."

"Excellent." The Riekan's smile held a false note to it. "Remember that feeling, because you won't experience it again."

He didn't see the syringe until after the needle pierced his skin. "What did you-?" Already, he felt like he was floating away

136

and heavier than a stone, all at the same time. "No, please," he begged, grabbing the doctor's lab coat.

"I have no choice, Mr. Alazar. You'll only make things worse if I let you live."

His body refused to obey his orders to get up and run, refused to voice the shout that was caught in his throat. And even as every muscle froze, every nerve ending felt flayed and raw, sending hot, maddening pain through his entire body. He couldn't move, couldn't scream, could do nothing to alleviate the terrible pain.

The intensity continued to climb, sending tears leaking from his immobile eyes. The Riekan man leaned over and looked at him, flicking a small penlight across each pupil. "Excellent," he muttered to himself again. "You will be dead soon, Mr. Alazar. And your whole cause will die with you. Berent has already seen to your friends."

No! He tried to speak, to move his tongue... but nothing happened. *Not Meris and the others. They can't be dead.*

A grin spread over the Riekan's face. "You're all alone and you will die in the most excruciating pain imaginable. I wish I could hear your screams, though. But I doubt you gave my son the dignity of hearing his before he died. Before you killed him."

The man's features hardened into a more typical Riekan expression and Darius thought the man would spit in his eyes. "His name was Jannik, and you and your insane followers cut him down like a dog! Part of me wants to rip you apart right now, but that would only end your suffering and I won't have that."

Darius could barely register everything he was saying now, but he latched onto the words as a lifeline to focus his mind on to ignore the pain. He would succeed for a single moment before the waves of agony would wash over him with renewed strength. *Please, God, make it stop! Please, just end it... take me from this...*

Unconsciousness was denied him. After a small eternity, his desperate breathing was stifled. His pounding heart slowed, stuttered.

Meris, I'm sorry.

His heart monitor emitted a single, insistent note.

CHAPTER 25 – MERIS

Wyll finally passed out ten minutes away from the city. "Why did it seem to hurt him so badly?" Meris asked Zac. "I mean, you got shot by Hauher's HEL-gun and we didn't know it until Myranda noticed the wound." They were seated on the Wardens' transporter's floor still, next to Wyll.

"Oh, it hurt plenty," Zac replied. "But it was a small area and some of the wound was deep enough to kill the nerve endings. I was lucky." He shrugged. "Any further in," he said, gesturing toward his midline, "and I would have been gored and died. Any shallower," he moved his finger to the surface of his side, "and I would have felt it a lot worse. Like Wyll." He tapped a spot on his side. "I've lost all feeling right there, where it was deepest."

She was still shaken by Wyll's screams; never had she heard cries of such pure agony. She shivered. "What did it feel like? Where you could feel it, I mean."

Zac's aqua eyes grew distant. "Like my nerves were on fire. Like... when you get a carpet burn or really bad sunburn, only multiplied by, like, a thousand." He shook his head and frowned at Wyll's unconscious form on the floor between them. "I can imagine the mind-breaking pain he felt."

Wyll's shirt – the blue and white one Leo had lent him – was ripped at an angle from his left shoulder to his right hip.

The edges of the material had singed and bit of it were melted into the wound. Blood seeped through the material here and there, but the wound was too shallow for serious bleeding. The flesh underneath looked like cooked steak. Smelled almost the same, too, a fact that she had desperately been trying to ignore.

The Tudoryan Warden, whose name they now knew was Fydach Cale, had used a numbing antibac spray on Wyll's back. He had apologized that he didn't have anything to treat the wound properly. He'd gone back to the cockpit area to co-pilot after that, but now he looked toward them again and said, "We're less than eight minutes out now. I radioed ahead several minutes ago to advise medical of your injuries. You will all receive treatment before taking the stand before the Council."

"Say again?" Edzard's voice nearly overlapped his co-pilot's. He listened to the comms device on his ear intently for a moment, then turned his head toward Fydach sharply. The Tudoryan's expression was grim in return. "Understood," Edzard replied. "Out."

"What is it?" Meris asked.

Edzard started flipping switches on the console. "You two should strap into the seats. We're starting the descent for landing."

"What about Wyll?" Zac asked.

"He'll be fine," Fydach assured him.

"Then so will we," Meris answered, settling against the seat behind her more and taking hold of Wyll's right arm.

Fydach grinned and made a sort of shrug with his head. "Suit yourselves."

"You didn't answer her question," Zac persisted. "What's wrong?"

The two Wardens exchanged a look. Eventually, Edzard said, "Someone has infiltrated the Infirmary. We're to take you directly to the Council Court instead until the perpetrator has been apprehended."

"Perpetrator?" The word sent chills over her body. "Perpetrator of what?"

"I don't know details, but it seems Darius Alazar has been attacked."

She heard Zac's sharp intake of breath. She herself couldn't breathe, couldn't move. If Alazar had been attacked, did that mean he was dead? Or would be soon? Had he had time to testify? Does this mean the Council is biased, somehow supporting Berent? How in the worlds had one of his people gotten inside?

"We'll know all the answers soon enough, I'd wager," Edzard said, making her realize she had asked all those questions out loud without realizing it. "Right now, we need to concentrate on getting you inside safely."

―――✕✝╫╲╲╪✝―――

As they slowed for landing, Meris glanced out the side door's window and saw the pale stone facade of the Court. Like the Courts on every other planet in the Newverse, this one was modeled after ancient cathedrals and fortresses of Earth – tall spires, pointed arches, flying buttresses, inner and outer crenellated walls, defensive artillery towers – and all crafted out of the pale cream marble-like Tudoryan carraigstone. The transporter was lowering down into the courtyard behind the Court's innermost wall. The wall rose high to their right, the Court itself loomed to their left. Before and behind, the North and South wings connected the main building to the inner wall first and then on to the outer wall.

The moment they touched down, Edzard and Fydach armed themselves with handguns and opened the PTV's side door cautiously. Once they saw the way was clear, Edzard helped Zac out while Meris and Fydach lifted Wyll onto the collapsible litter stowed behind the passenger seats and carried him out. The Wardens led them across the courtyard and through the massive, pointed arch double-doorway to the North wing. The doors were made of heavy ironwood, reinforced with an intricate design of wrought iron.

The massive doors parted soundlessly and Meris found herself and her friends facing a long carraigstone corridor, arched just like the doors, but otherwise plain and a little oppressive. Edzard and Fydach led them down this hall until it intersected with a much larger, much more impressive one. They took a left into this larger hall, which was also arched carraigstone with huge glass panels lining the whole way. The middle was dotted by tall balcony railings overlooking the floor below.

Wyll came to slowly and silently but Meris could see the pain and anger in his eyes when they turned toward her. He groaned. "Are we there?"

"We're here," she told him. "But we're not safe. Darius has been attacked." Meris took a moment to shift her grip on the litter's handles, remembering a time not so long ago when she and Myranda had carried Alazar out of Stell-Ore in much the same way. At least her shoulder didn't hurt this time.

Please, let him be alive.

Wyll closed his eyes and she thought he'd passed out. But then he opened them again and said, "Let me up."

"Wyll, you need-"

"Let me up, Meris."

She sighed. "Warden Cale, Wyll wants to walk."

Cale gave her a dubious look over his shoulder but stopped and lowered the litter to the floor. He and Meris helped Wyll to his feet. "Are you okay?" she asked him.

He tested his back muscles gingerly then gave her a nod. They continued to a short flight of steps and across an intersecting hall. They had to go up another small flight of steps on the far side and on a short way to another intersection. A collection of towering carraigstone columns supported an airy spire over their heads. They took another left here, then right as the hallway turned sharply and became a plain corridor much like the one they'd first entered, only instead of being lit by recessed overhead lights, this one's illumination came from cut glass lamps lining each side in an alternating pattern. It was pretty but distracting.

This corridor was intersected by multiple hallways, and each one they passed was filled with people – staff of the Court, Wardens, and Enforcers – coming and going about their business with urgent efficiency. A pair of Enforcers accompanying a man who was in leg and wrist shackles and wearing what looked like a muzzle waited for them to pass by before entering the hall behind them at a careful distance.

She hadn't gotten a clean look at the man, but the impression she got from his coloring and bearing was that he might be Riekan or Minosian. If so, she wondered if this was the man who had attacked Darius. She was aching to know if he was alive or not, whether he had gotten to testify or had been silenced before he could. If the latter, she vowed even more firmly than before that she would see Berent held accountable for all his atrocities, no matter the cost.

They turned right down another hallway, wide and dotted on their left by tall stained-glass windows. This corridor ended in a wide-open space whose opposite wall held a set of enormous carraigstone doors, flanked by twelve guards, six on each side.

Edzard relieved himself of Zac and approached the guards. They spoke a challenge in some sort of code that sounded like random words to her, and he replied in, apparently, the correct sequence because they relaxed their stance. One opened a smaller door inset the larger one on the right and slipped through. A moment later, he returned and beckoned toward them.

Edzard nodded and came back to help Zac once more. The larger doors parted to reveal the Council Court to them for the first time. Meris gaped unabashedly at the brightness, the cleanliness and the sheer... authority the huge room exuded. The floor, walls and rib-vaulted ceilings were all carraigstone, pure and almost glowing in the bright light. And then she saw why: the enormous, faceted crystal suspended above the room magnified the light emitted by dozens of warm white lamps set high on the walls beneath a multitude of windows.

"Wow," she sighed.

Zac, now standing next to her, shivered. "Yeah. More intimidating than I even imagined."

To their left and right rose tiered seating in warm-toned wood. The seats were filled with people from every planet in the Newverse. They all shifted and leaned forward to get a better look at the new arrivals. But Meris' eyes were drawn directly ahead of them to the Council Adjudicators.

They were seated in massive thrones on a raised platform, making them peer down at her and her friends from behind their podium. Their robes were each a different color, signifying what planet they represented. What caught her attention next were the witness boxes. Witness cages, more like. Steel bars forming a cell on top of high stone pillars with steps cut into the bases leading to them. Standing next to each box was a black robe-clad Barrister – a Court Agent that acted as a sort of lawyer or mediator.

"These are the ones we've sought?" the Sindrian Adjudicator asked. She peered down at them regally, like a queen rather than a judge.

"Yes, your Honor," Edzard answered. "They come to speak for Darius Alazar."

Meris tore her gaze from the Adjudicator to Edzard and then back. "Please, my friends are hurt. They need medical treatment. And I need to know if Alazar is alive. I need-"

"Silence," the brown-robed Minosian Adjudicator said, his voice sharp like breaking glass.

The Sindrian Adjudicator held up a hand. "They have the right to ask. And to be treated." She gestured to a Sendrassan man seated on the lowest tier, who hurried forward carrying a metal case. "But first, Miss Brand, you will tell us the... abridged version of your story while the Infirmary is secured."

The little man opened the case and removed a syringe. He brought it to Meris. "You will need to roll up your sleeve."

"Why? What are you going to do with that?"

He looked confused. "They don't know, either, it would seem, Your Honors."

Zac tried to pull away from Edzard. "We don't know what, either?"

The Sindrian judge sighed. "This is what happens when protocol is not adhered to. If you all would have been processed properly, your counselors would have prepared you for this."

"What is this?" Wyll asked.

"Colloquially, it is what you might call truth serum," the ebony-skinned Egalian Adjudicator in dark blue robes explained, the expression on his broad face one of impatience. "Not how we refer to it, of course, but that is the gist of its purpose. You will receive the injection in order to testify. No injection, no testimony. Understood?"

"Like hell," Zac muttered. "How do we know that's what it really is? I mean, we hear Alazar was attacked inside your own Infirmary and you want us to trust that what you're gonna inject us with is what you say it is just because you said that's what it was?"

"Insubordinate fool!" the Riekan Adjudicator said hatefully.

"He has a point," the Egalian Adjudicator replied.

"You're only agreeing with him because he's Egalian," the Riekan Adjudicator accused.

"And you're only against him because you're a Riekan," the Egalian replied, raising his eyebrow and tilting his head as if hitting a tennis ball back into his colleague's side of the court.

"Enough!" The Sindrian judge made a choppy gesture of her thin hand. To Meris and Zac, she made a conceding dip of her head. "Your concerns are valid. And I admit that I have no way of proving ourselves to you to lay them to rest."

"You can start by telling us whether or not Alazar's alive," Wyll said.

She turned to the other six and they each nodded in turn. "Darius Alazar was found unresponsive by one of our nurses just before you arrived. We were told that the medical team has been doing what they can to revive him."

Meris gasped. "Unresponsive... But now? Do you know if he's still alive now?" Meris asked, trembling as tears filled her eyes.

"We have not been given any updates yet." She frowned. "All we know was that he was injected with something, but without the culprit in custody, the doctors don't know what they're fighting. Please accept the Council's apologies and believe me when I tell you we will apprehend the person responsible. Especially if Mr. Alazar should succumb."

Zac's face darkened with grief and anger. His hands had clenched into fists. "Do you even know who it was? How did this happen? Here, of all places?"

Several of the Adjudicators shifted uneasily in their seats, some leaning forward as if to defend themselves, but the Sindrian Adjudicator raised her hand to silence them. "Trust me, Officer Colphin, we intend to discover the answer of how this could happen. And yes, we have surveillance footage of the Riekan doctor who attacked him and have Enforcers and Wardens searching the building for him. He will not get away with this."

Meris could not stop the tears from burning their way down her cheeks. So many lost, and now, if Darius died... What point was there to any of this anymore?

No, Berent still needed to pay. Ellias and his crew – and Myranda and Leo – still needed justice.

"Thank you," she told the judge, wiping her tears away. "I appreciate you being honest with us." She turned to the Sendrassan. "I'll take the serum."

CHAPTER 26 – MERIS

The Sendrassan man raised the syringe and his other hand toward Meris. She offered her arm and he took her hand gently, raising her sleeve. They locked eyes once more and she nodded.

"Wait," Zac interjected. "Meris, let me go first." He shrugged. "Just in case."

The Sendrassan man gave his own shrug and moved past Meris to Zac. He tapped the barrel and squeezed a few drops of the liquid out to clear any air that may have been in the syringe. Then, when Zac offered his arm, he plunged the needle into his skin and emptied the syringe's contents into his system. Zac gritted his teeth and shook his arm.

"Burns a little," he told her. "But I'm okay."

She gave him a small smile, then turned her attention to the Sendrassan. "What about Wyll? He's in no condition to testify."

Wyll cleared his throat. His voice was thick with grief and strained with the lingering pain but sounded strong. "I'll be fine, Meris." He sniffed, holding out his arm to the Sendrassan. "This is what we came here to do." He, too, frowned and shook his arm after the injection, but gave her a reassuring nod.

"Now is it my turn?" Meris asked him with an exasperated air.

The Sendrassan prepared a third syringe and jabbed it into her arm. The sensation as the drug entered her bloodstream was like when a numbed limb regains feeling, a tiny prickling, buzzing effect. Almost immediately, a burning sensation followed, but only for a few seconds. She shook her arm and then almost gasped as the drug took effect. She felt alert but calm, and there was a slight detachment between herself and her more powerful emotions. Even the overwhelming grief of a moment ago dulled to a smoldering sadness.

"Are you all ready?" the Sindrian Adjudicator asked.

"We are," Wyll answered for them.

"Then climb the steps to the box."

Meris calmly ascended while Edzard and Fydach assisted Zac and Wyll up the steps behind her. At the top, their Barrister – an Egalian man in his early fifties – opened the cage and let them pass into it. She discovered a bench in the middle of the cage, and she gestured for her friends to take a seat. Wyll and Zac sank onto it with audible groans. Edzard and Fydach left them then, returning to the floor below to wait. After a moment, the Barrister turned to the Council.

When each Adjudicator nodded, he turned to face her. "Meris Brand."

"Yes?"

"You were speaking with Ellias Gammett, the crew chief of Cartage 15 when he and his entire crew were slaughtered before your very eyes, were you not?"

"I was." She answered without thinking, but the images of that day were tumbling around in her mind: the crimson spray of Ellias' blood across the snow, his fear and grief as he watched his men die, the sound of the drill head lifting and pouring tons of Bolidium onto the unsuspecting miners...Wyll's masked face staring at her through the vid-phone.

"And who was it that killed Ellias Gammett and his crew?"

"Wyll Meiryg." Again, she answered without thought, without hesitation. "But it was on the orders of-"

"And who does Wyll Meiryg work for?"

"Darius Alazar." The spectators murmured. The Adjudicators leaned forward or stroked their beards or chins or otherwise expressed interest. "But it was Commander Hauher who gave the order, not Darius." She felt relieved to have gotten this out before the Barrister cut her off again. Wyll gave her a grateful smile.

"And you know this how?"

"Wyll told me. And Darius told me he did not give any such order." She knew talking about Darius should have her wracked with grief and worry. It was there, but she felt detached from it.

"I see. Wyll Meiryg."

"Yes, sir?" Wyll painfully stood at attention. Meris stayed by his side in case he needed her support, physical or otherwise.

"Is Commander Hauher your immediate superior?"

"He is."

"And he gave you the order to murder the crew of Cartage 15?"

Wyll's eyes grew troubled. "Yes. He gave the order to initiate the Sanitizing Protocol because he said they had contracted a brain-bug."

"And what is this protocol?"

"We have orders to neutralize anyone known to have been infected with any off-world illness."

"Neutralize. You mean kill?"

"Yes."

"And who came up with this protocol?"

"I don't know, sir."

Murmurs flitted through those gathered to watch. The Egalian Barrister's eyebrows drew down sharply. "You don't know? And yet you did not hesitate to carry it out when ordered to?"

"No. I was trained-"

"Trained? By whom?"

"Commander Hauher."

"Commander Hauher trained you to kill the employees of Stell-Ore when ordered to, without question?" Again, murmurs rippled through the room.

"He did. It is a safety protocol. If a crew is infected with a brain-bug or other illness and is allowed to come back to Sindria, there is a good chance the entire population would be exposed and at risk. We are sent to neutralize the threat before it can reach this planet or others."

"And were you trained to recognize the symptoms of someone exposed to a brain-bug, as he said this crew had been?"

"A little. We know some of the signs, as a precaution, in case we ourselves get exposed when carrying out the protocol."

"And did you see Ellias Gammett or any member of the crew of Cartage 15 exhibit any of these signs or symptoms?"

"I did not have the time to assess them myself. I was told they were infected. I was told to carry out the protocol. I went to Thalassa and I carried out the protocol. Then I returned to Sindria."

"So, you did not try to confirm that the crew was, indeed, infected before you murdered them?"

Wyll flinched. "No."

Meris felt tears flood her eyes, and she knew Wyll wanted to soften the blow of what he was saying, but was unable to, thanks to the serum. He touched her arm; Zac squeezed her hand.

"But you now know that they were not, after all, infected, don't you, Lieutenant Meiryg?"

"Yes. Now I do. I know that what Commander Hauher told me was a lie. I now know that he and Berent Gaehts worked together to overthrow Darius Alazar and take over Stell-Ore."

"What proof have you to back up these claims?" This came from the Riekan Adjudicator.

Wyll opened his mouth, then shut it and turned to Zac and Meris. "Commander Hauher admitted as much," Zac said. "He led the attacks on those of us who supported Alazar."

"But Commander Hauher is dead now, isn't he? You and Lieutenant Meiryg killed him before leaving Stell-Ore with Darius Alazar. Isn't that correct?" the Riekan Adjudicator continued, addressing Wyll.

"Yes, it is, but-"

"So, you cannot prove that Commander Hauher and Berent Gaehts used you to enact a coup to overthrow Darius Alazar and take over Stell-Ore, can you?" The Riekan Adjudicator leaned forward.

"Prove? No. But what I'm telling you is true. The serum-"

"The serum only makes you tell us what you believe to be true," The Minosian Adjudicator interjected, with an air of someone tired of repeating themselves. "Facts and evidence are still preferred over testimony."

"What I believe? What I believe to be true is that Berent Gaehts is a monster. He killed my best friend, Amund Halsin, my sister- his wife- Myranda Gaehts, and our friend Leo Hull. And he tried to kill me and my friends here with me. He is responsible for the atrocities at Stell-Ore. Him. Not me, not Darius Alazar – Berent Gaehts." The vehemence in his voice was muted to what he must be feeling, but it was unmistakable, nonetheless.

"He did kill Myranda Gaehts," Zac added. "I was there. I saw it."

"I was there, too," Meris said, tearing up again. "He tried to kill me, and Myranda saved my life by taking the airbolt meant for me. Berent needs to be brought to justice for that."

The Riekan Adjudicator raised his eyebrows. "Passionate words. But again, I ask you all: What proof do you have of any of this?"

"What about the security feeds from Stell-Ore?" Wyll asked.

"Corrupted, conveniently," the purple-robed Pentarian Adjudicator said with a bored air as she appeared to examine her grey fingernails.

"Enough," the Sindrian Adjudicator said, her voice heavy with authority. "Let the Barrister do his job."

"Thank you, Your Honor," the Barrister at their cage said. "Yes, much of the security feed was corrupted. However, what does remain seems to suggest there is more to the story than you are telling. For instance, did you not gas an entire floor of your fellow security officers and break Darius Alazar free from where he was being held pending investigation?"

"We rescued him from Berent!" Meris said. "He was beaten nearly to death by Berent and his men. There was no 'pending investigation.' He would have died if we hadn't gotten him out of there."

"And in doing so, you murdered at least one of those security officers, did you not, Zac Colphin?"

"He deserved it." Another murmur rippled through the Council and spectators. "He opened fire on us first; he killed Jenna Avelin. It was self-defense and the defense of my comrades and Meris Brand, Myranda Gaehts, and Darius Alazar. It was not murder."

"That is for the Council to decide, Officer Colphin. Not you," the green-robed Tudoryan Adjudicator said.

"All due respect, sir, but the Council was not there. We were attacked. I defended us. It was kill or be killed."

The Council members kept their faces carefully neutral. But Meris thought that, contrary to her fears, Zac's words made a positive impact on the Adjudicators. The Barrister, however, was not convinced.

"Kill or be killed. So now we live in a savage society like the animals, is that it, Officer Colphin? Or like back on Earth?" Zac started to speak, but the Barrister held up a hand to silence him.

"Myranda's tablet," Meris said. She reached into the pocket of the pants she borrowed while at Leo's. They had been his, adjusted to her size. It was impossible to believe he was dead now.

"Excuse me?" The Barrister arched an eyebrow at her.

"We never saw what she had on it. She said she discovered on her own that Berent was behind the murders of Ellias and his crew. But we never looked at her proof." She turned to the Council. "Will you allow us to show you what she found?"

The Council members conferred via a screen and keypad set into the arm of their throne-like chairs. After a long moment, the Sindrian Adjudicator looked up and steepled her fingers. "We will recess to view the contents of the tablet. We will make our decision after that."

The Council adjourned for the time being and Edzard and Fydach led them back out of the box and down the steps. At the bottom, they were flanked by another pair of Wardens and escorted through a door next to the tier of seating to the Council's left. The door opened into a narrow passage to another door, this one leading them into a small anteroom. It was sparsely furnished, but comfortable, with a plush settee on either side and a low table bearing a bowl of fruit next to one. Famished, they each immediately grabbed some of the fruit and ate hungrily. Meris noticed when her hand brushed the edge of the bowl that it felt like it had been affixed to the table. Apparently, someone had been worried that a desperate prisoner might try to execute a daring escape by defeating highly trained Wardens or Enforcers with a fruit bowl.

A gesture from Edzard sent the two extra Wardens out of the room. Meris turned to him. "I don't think I properly thanked you for saving our lives," she said, holding out her hand with a smile.

He looked at her, his expression neither soft nor hard. "I was doing my job, Miss Brand. Please don't mistake it for anything else."

Her smile fell, as did her hand. But what he said was fair enough. He saved them in order to bring them before the Court, but that did not make them friends. "I can see why Yerna told us to only trust you," she told him with a sad half-smile. "You are as objective as they come."

His dispassionate mien faltered. "She said that?"

Meris nodded. "Her last words were 'Trust Edzard. Only Edzard.'"

He took a moment and then said. "We cannot take your friends to the Infirmary, now that it's been compromised, but I can have a doctor see to them here. I know of one, at least, that we can trust."

Fydach shifted slightly toward them. "Ed," he warned.

"They have a right to receive medical treatment while they are in these walls," he replied quietly. "The Council promised them aid. We are bound by the laws of safekeeping."

Fydach sighed but nodded. "That we are. Find a doctor, I will stay with them."

Edzard nodded and started for the door. Meris took a step toward him. "Wait." He turned back to her. She eyed Fydach a moment before saying, "Yerna told me to trust only you. Do you trust him with our lives?"

Fydach's eyes narrowed. "I *saved* your lives."

"So did Lilla," she told him, sounding much calmer than she felt. "And then when she got us far enough away from the city, she tried to kill us. She killed Yerna."

Edzard stepped in to interrupt Fydach before he could retort any further. "They've learned the hard way what it means to trust the wrong people – can you blame them for being more careful now?" Then, to Meris, he said, "Yes. I trust him with my life and yours. I will return with a doctor I know we can trust as well."

"Okay," Meris said.

Edzard lifted his eyebrows at Fydach. "Yes?"

Fydach nodded.

"Don't let anyone in but me. Verification code: Opal Violet," Edzard instructed as he left.

An awkward silence descended on the room. Meris kept her eyes down and shifted uneasily. Fydach sighed and moved to stand in front of the door.

"I meant no offense," she offered after a moment. "But he was right, we don't know who to trust anymore. And with this place getting infiltrated and our friend possibly murdered... I just don't want anyone else to get hurt or die because of me."

Fydach was looking past her resolutely and she thought he might not answer. With a shrugging flap of her hands against her thighs, she turned back and sat next to Wyll on the settee. As soon as she was seated, Fydach said, "For what it's worth-"

A sudden, urgent knocking on the door interrupted him. He frowned and turned, putting his hand on the doorknob but not turning it. "Yes?"

"Warden Cale?"

"Yes."

"Please, you must come quickly!"

Wyll was on his feet and moved next to the table, his stance ready for a fight. "Who is that?"

Fydach turned his head back toward him and shook it. He mouthed, Be ready. Then he turned back to the door. "Identify yourself and report."

"I am Warden Fyntan Blair. Sir, please, I need you to come with me."

"I have orders from Warden Kier not to open this door for anyone but him."

"But that's just it, sir, Warden Kier's been injured. He's asking for you."

For just a split second, Fydach stiffened and his hand clenched on the doorknob as if he were going to open the door. But, after turning to look back at Meris and her friends, he stepped away and activated his comms. "Cale to Kier, report." He kept his voice low enough that the person outside the room couldn't hear.

No answer.

"Kier, advise your status."

Silence.

Fydach went back to the door. Wyll stepped in front of him. "What are you doing?"

"Step aside."

"You don't know who that is out there. You open that door, you could be killing all of us."

"I'm not opening the door. Step aside." He nudged Wyll aside and pressed his ear against the door, listening intently. "Warden Blair, is it?"

"Yes, sir. Please, you must hurry." The voice outside the door was getting impatient.

"What verification code did Warden Kier give?"

There was a pause that lasted just a moment too long from the visitor outside. "He- he's very badly hurt. He gave no code before blacking out. He just said, 'get Cale,' sir."

"And you just left him where he was, unprotected? Was the person who attacked him still around? Did you search for the perpetrator? Did you secure the scene? Did you verify that he had assistance from the medical staff? Who is your superior officer? What is your identification number?"

Again, there was a moment of silence on the other side. But when it was broken this time, it was by a loud thump on the door. Fydach jumped back, holding out his hands to warn them to stay away. Meris helped Zac up off the settee and she and her comrades backed toward the opposite wall. Another loud thump jarred the door.

"They'd need a battering ram to get through," Fydach assured them.

Another thump landed hard and they could see the door shudder, but, as their Warden said, it held. There was a shout, like a challenge given, followed by a quick exchange of gunfire. It was quiet again for a second or two, then someone pounded on the door, causing Meris to jump with fright.

"Opal Violet," Edzard said on the other side of the door. "Let me in, Fyd."

With a relieved sigh, Fydach opened the door. Edzard and a Sendrassan doctor entered. The doctor looked shaken, his dark eyes wide and his pale skin even paler. Edzard looked angry.

"What happened?" Fydach demanded. "You weren't answering your comms."

"We were ambushed, I lost my comms in the scuffle. The infiltration is much more extensive than one aggrieved Riekan doctor. Berent's supporters are everywhere." He looked at Meris and her friends. "Berent was captured not long after I shot him down. He's been brought here to stand trial as well, but those loyal to him have flooded in, intent on breaking him free. It's a free-for-all out there."

"Berent's here? He's in custody?" Wyll asked.

"For the time being, yes."

The three of them exchanged relieved grins. But Meris had another thought. "What about Darius?" Meris asked. "Did he testify before... before he was attacked?"

"He did, yes," the doctor answered. "He gave a short testimony before being brought down to us for treatment."

"Thank God," Wyll said, letting out a slow breath. "His testimony and Myranda's tablet will seal Berent's fate."

The doctor looked at Wyll a little more closely. "Young man, what happened to you?"

Wyll looked up sharply. "Me? A couple of transporter crashes, a few fistfights and a HEL-gun gash on my back. I'll be all right."

"Wyll, you're not all right," Meris argued.

"Zac's hurt worse than I am."

The Sendrassan doctor looked at Zac, seeing the cuts and gashes on his face, arms, and torso, then down at the mangled leg that hung uselessly from his hip. The doctor's eyes went wide. "You were forced to testify with your leg like that? The Council will hear from me about this, I can tell you that."

"Can you help him?" Meris asked.

The doctor tore his gaze from the leg and looked at her. "Not here." He turned back to Zac. "Son, I fear that leg may not be salvageable. I don't even know how you're conscious right now, with the damage and the infection that's set in."

"Infection?" Zac glanced down at his leg. "I didn't even know..." He jerked his head back up. "What are you saying, 'may not be salvageable'?"

Now that she looked more closely, she could see he was pale and a sheen of sweat coated his skin. What she had thought was stress from the pain he was in, she now knew was his body reacting to the fever that must be raging inside it. The doctor was right, Zac should be unconscious.

"I'll have to get in there and look to be sure," the doctor answered, "but I believe we'll need to amputate if we're going to save your life." He looked to Edzard and Fydach. "And we need to do it now. In the OR. Can you get us there?"

Fydach turned to Edzard, his eyebrow raised in question. Edzard nodded. "We can. If we take the side halls," he added to Fydach.

"Amputate?" Zac's question was barely audible.

Fydach looked like he wanted to protest, but then must have decided Edzard was right. He pulled a slim device – much like the one Wyll had used in the Stell-Ore compound to override door locks and cameras – from his pocket and pressed a button. A panel in the wall next to the settee on the left side of the room slid open, barely wide enough for two people to fit through. He stepped into the passage and switched on a strip of lights halfway up the wall.

"Clear," he reported to Edzard.

"Everyone inside."

Wyll went in first, then Meris supporting Zac, then Edzard, who closed the panel by pressing another switch on the wall. The passage was constructed of concrete, plain and utilitarian, and somewhat cramped. Meris and Zac had to angle themselves to both fit between the confines. The lights in the strips lining both walls were a bright warm amber color that was easy on the eyes after the cooler-colored lighting of the anteroom and Council Court.

Eventually, the passage branched off into multiple routes, but Fydach never hesitated in choosing his path. The air was a little too still, and Meris soon found herself panting and beads of sweat had sprung up on her skin and Zac's. His hand in hers over her shoulder was clammy and his breathing was becoming labored.

"Are you all right?" Meris asked him quietly. She felt the need to whisper in this place.

"I think I'm running on fumes right now," he murmured.

"I'm sorry, Zac. I just wish this was all over. I wish I could undo all of it."

"I know you do. We all feel the same way. But it's not your fault, remember that. No matter what else happens here today, remember that none of it was your fault."

She shivered, despite the stuffiness of the tunnel. His words sounded so... final. Just like with Darius.

CHAPTER 27 – WYLL

The tunnel went on forever. Or so it seemed. But eventually, Warden Cale led them through another panel in the wall that opened out into a small room much like the one they'd left behind, only this one had individual chairs and a counter with cabinets, a sink, and a beverage dispenser in the corner behind the door. It was empty of other people at the moment. Wyll immediately turned to help Meris bring Zac through.

"Stay here," Cale warned, going to the door and peering through it. He glanced back at them for a second before returning his gaze through the doorway. "It's clear here. I'll scout ahead. Obsidian jade." He told Kier.

"Copy. I'll stay with them."

Kier slipped through the door, closing it behind him. In the distance, shouting and the occasional sharp cries of pain echoed through the halls. Wyll's hands clenched into fists. If only he had his armor and weapons.

Zac was fading fast. Adrenaline from the attack earlier had kept him going long after exhaustion should have knocked him flat, but that had to be wearing off now. Especially with the serum's calming effect. Wyll's own reserves of energy were depleted; the need for justice and vindication were the only things keeping him going.

"While we're waiting," the doctor said as he approached Wyll, "let me take a look at your back."

Wyll took one of the chairs that didn't have arms and pulled it more into the middle of the floor where he could sit backward on it. Behind him, he heard the doctor gasp and say, "Lord above! The two of you should be in hospital right now."

Wyll's heart did a little jump. "Is it that bad?" He tried looking over his shoulder, but that movement pulled on the skin of his back painfully. Cale's numbing agent was starting to wear off, apparently.

"This needs debrided, sanitized, and sealed."

"Can't we just throw some more antibac and numbing agent on it and call it done?"

"Young man, the shirt you are wearing has melted into your skin. If it is not removed, it will fester."

"Then let's get it removed." Before anyone could stop him, and before the numbing went away totally, he pulled the front of the shirt up, wriggling his arms out and sliding it carefully over his head.

Everyone sucked in a collective sharp breath, including him, as the shirt fell to hang from his back. He started to reach back and yank on the tattered material, but the doctor shot out a hand to stop him. "No! You'll only make it worse."

"We don't have time for delicate here, Doctor," Wyll said. "There's a fight going on out there, and I'm a soldier. I need to get this off so I can defend myself and my friends." With that, he grabbed a wad of the material and pulled.

A terrible ripping pain seared across his back once more, making his head swim and his stomach roil in protest. Vaguely, he heard Meris yell his name and the doctor telling him to stop, but that was all background to the throbbing pain that filled his awareness. He felt blood well up and run down his back.

The doctor muttered chastisements under his breath as he rushed to the sink in the corner to run water onto a stack of paperex towels and hurried back to start bathing the wound. Wyll hissed in a breath several times as the doctor worked to undo the damage he'd done to himself.

There was a knock on the door. "Obsidian jade," Cale's muffled voice announced.

Kier opened the door, ushering in his comrade, who wheeled in a hover wheelchair. He stopped short as he took in the scene before him. "What happened?"

"Wyll decided to do a little doctoring on himself," Zac said.

"Ah." Cale turned his attention to the doctor. "The OR is secure. But we need to get Officer Colphin there now."

"Uh... all right," the doctor said. His hand had paused in its ministrations.

"You see to Zac," Meris said, "I'll see to Wyll. As best I can, anyway."

"There should be a med kit in one of the cabinets to get him by until I can properly treat him," the doctor told her. "As for clothing..."

"I can secure that for him," Kier said.

"Right then," Wyll said, "that's all settled. Zac?" He shifted on the chair until he could see his comrade. He held out his hand. Zac took it and they clasped wrists. "I'll see you on the other side of this thing, brother."

There were tears in Zac's eyes. "Yes, sir, Lieutenant. You watch your back out here," he added with a wink.

Wyll grinned. "Maybe I'll do a better job of it this time, hey?"

Meris squeezed Zac in a fierce hug once he'd released Wyll's hand. "I'm praying for you," she told him, her voice choked with tears.

"I'll see you again soon, Meris," Zac replied, but from the expression on his face, Wyll could tell he wasn't entirely convinced that was true. Zac was worried, scared.

And so was Wyll.

Cale touched the doctor's arm and nodded toward Zac. The doctor cleared his throat and laid a hand on Zac's shoulder. "Come on, son, we need to move."

"Right," Zac said, looking at each of them in turn one more time. "So, I guess I'll see you all later." He gave them a shaky smile and then let the doctor help him follow Cale out the door.

Wyll and Meris exchanged worried looks. Kier watched them a moment, then said, "It shouldn't take long. And we have top of the line prosthetics. Physically, he'll be fine, but the loss of a limb can have a profound effect, even with a prosthesis."

Wyll nodded. "Zac is a soldier. We've been conditioned to accept the possibility of ending up maimed ever since we joined up. But I know him, and this is going to be devastating. At least at first. He'll adjust soon enough, though."

Over the next half hour, Meris continued to wash the wounds on his back, apologizing every time he winced. When she was satisfied it was clean enough, she found the med kit and applied numbing antibac and gel seals. Once the last seal was in place, he stood and gingerly tested flexing and twisting to see if they held and if he had any pain. With a sigh of relief, he faced her.

"Thank you. Good as new, or at least good enough for now." She gave him a smile, but her eyes told him she was miles away in her thoughts. "Are you all right?"

"Sorry. I don't do well with waiting like this. Do you think something's happened to Zac?"

"It's only been thirty minutes. He's getting a limb amputated. Even with all our advanced medicine, these things take time to fix."

"You're right. I know you are. I just can't help worrying, thinking something's going to go wrong and Berent will win."

"And I thought you were the one who had all the faith."

"I am. I do, but - No, you're right. I just have to have faith." She smiled. "Thank you."

"You just needed a reminder."

"No, Wyll – thank you. For everything. I couldn't have come this far without you. None of us could."

"Actually, none of us would have to be here if it weren't for me."

"That's not-"

"You heard what the Barrister said. All I would have had to do was wait just a few minutes, watched Ellias and his crew, and I would have seen they weren't infected." He rubbed his hands down his face. "I wouldn't have killed them all and Berent wouldn't have been able to take over Stell-Ore."

"But you would have disobeyed a direct order. You would have been court-martialed or whatever they do-"

"The Hole. I would have been sentenced to The Hole." He felt cold even thinking about it.

"Oh. That's... that's terrible. For how long?"

"However long Hauher saw fit."

She knelt next to him. "Are you saying there wouldn't have been a trial or some sort of investigation first? He'd just throw you in there and walk away?"

"Yes. Exactly that."

"That's barbaric! And illegal, it has to be."

"Probably. But Ellias and his men would be alive. Amund would be alive. Jenna would be alive. Leo," tears filled his eyes. "So many dead. Because of me."

She took his hand in hers. "Because of Berent and Hauher. Not you."

He felt the tears threatening to fall and tried to smile through them. "I appreciate what you're trying to do, but I am as much to blame." He sniffled. "I just want this to be over. I – I just wish we could start over," he said, his voice choked with emotion.

Meris hugged him carefully. "I know," she said, sniffling.

He wrapped his arms around her. "I just want my sister back." His voice broke as a sob tore from him before he could stop it.

She held him until the worst of it passed, just as he had done for her in the forest. But when he could compose himself, he dried his eyes and turned to Kier. He cleared his throat and asked, "You mentioned clothing being available nearby?"

He had been looking away to give them some privacy, but now he turned to them and nodded. "In the next room over." He eyed the door. 'It shouldn't take long to grab something. I will be right back. You two stay put."

He went to the door and grabbed the handle. As soon as he opened it, a Minosian Enforcer was standing there, her hand poised to knock on the door herself. She stepped back, startled.

Kier paused, his body tensing up. "What is it?" he asked.

"I've come to let you know these two are being released. The Council has reviewed their testimony."

Something felt off. "What happened to the hearing? What will happen to Berent?"

"That is no longer your concern, Lieutenant Meiryg. You may leave. Now." The caramel-brown skin of her face looked sculpted out of the finest clay, so emotionless was she as she said this.

"But I don't understand," Meris insisted. "So, we just walk out of here and wait to hear the outcome like everyone else on the street? I mean, this is ridiculous- we brought you the truth, we brought you the evidence against Berent. We should be allowed to stay and see this through." She drew herself up to her full, if unimpressive, height. "We're staying."

"Such courage and passion," the Enforcer said, a sneer tugging at her thin lips as she drew a baton from a loop at her hip. "However, that is not an option. Warden," she made a gesture as if for Kier to step aside.

"This makes no sense," Wyll said, rising from the chair.

"No, it doesn't," Kier said. His hand flashed to his gun and drew it, but before he could take aim, the Minosian squinted her dark eyes in a snarl and whacked the baton into Kier's throat.

He dropped to his knees, choking, the gun falling from his grip. She shut the door and strode past him. "Run," Wyll told Meris, placing himself between her and the attacker.

The Minosian lunged at Wyll, striking out at his chest with the baton. He stumbled back, the breath knocked from his lungs momentarily. The Warden then struck Meris as she tried to dodge past, sending her sprawling back on the floor. But then Wyll was in the fray, knocking the Minosian's legs out from under her. She did not go down for long, however, but pushed herself up onto her feet before she landed fully on the floor.

Meris, he noticed, had gotten to her feet and grabbed the med kit. She hurled it at the Minosian just as she stepped in for another swing at Wyll. The kit did little damage, but it served as a distraction. One that allowed Wyll to strike at her unguarded midsection. She doubled over, gasping, and Meris slipped past her to the door.

He squared his stance and pressed his advantage, kicking the Minosian's leg at the knee. A sickening crunch and her scream was his reward. He also heard Meris tear the door open and shout for help. Moments later, a Sindrian Warden with skin almost as pale as his white-blonde hair rushed in and brought his baton down hard on the Minosian's head as she and Wyll grappled again. She crumpled like a rag doll, and Wyll had a flashback to seeing Myranda fall. He staggered back, expecting the next blow to land on him. Instead, the Sindrian used his restraints to cuff the intruder's hands and feet.

"Are you all right?"

Wyll, panting from exertion, nodded. "I'll live." He looked for Meris but didn't see her. "Meris?"

"The short Sindrian gal?"

"That's right," he replied with a smile.

"She's fine. Getting Warden Kier some help." He stood and offered his hand. "Warden Halden Riis."

Wyll shook his hand. "Lieutenant Wyll Meiryg, Stell-Ore Security. Thanks for the assist."

He nodded with a smile. "Come with me, I'll get you someplace safe."

"As much as I appreciate the offer, safe isn't exactly where I want to be."

"All right. Let's go find your little friend."

Alazar, Zac – they could be in trouble. "Wait – if we were attacked, our friends in the Surgical Ward may have been targeted as well."

He nodded once. "To the ORs it is, then."

"Lead the way."

After a quick stop to the room next door to get a new shirt – a plain grey one with long sleeves and 'Infirmary' stenciled on the back – he followed the Sindrian down the hall to a waiting room and nurses station. A few nurses and orderlies seemed upset by something, and everyone was rushing around. The Sindrian Warden stopped a nurse as she brisked by.

"The other witnesses in the Stell-Ore case, the ones brought here for treatment, where are they?"

She gave him and Wyll a sorrowful look. "I'm afraid you're both too late. The Infirmary has been overrun. Everyone's dead. Almost everyone," she corrected, her ebony skin crinkling as her forehead furrowed. "We're evacuating survivors but there's so many invading soldiers blocking our routes. I'm sorry," she said, rushing away.

Wyll felt like he'd been punched in the gut – again. "No," he said.

Not them, too. Without Alazar, this whole thing could end up being for nothing. And Zac should not have been in any serious danger. The wound to his leg had been catastrophic in many ways, yes, but with the surgery, he would have been fine. If Berent's supporters hadn't gotten to him. He would have been fine...

Oh, please, God, not Zac, too. He ran a shaky hand over his face and sighed. The burden of one more life lost weighed on him unbearably.

Riis gave him a sympathetic grimace. "I'm sorry, Lieutenant."

"I have to find them. I have to find Meris before she – Is there a morgue? Someplace where the casualties would be taken?"

"Yes, but there's no way to know if the way is clear or if they'd even have been removed from the battlefield yet."

Battlefield. *Welcome to your war...* "I have to look anyway. Do we need a keycard? Should we find the nurse again?"

"No need," Riis said, "I'm authorized. Follow me."

As they rushed through a veritable maze of hallways, they passed other nurses and doctors rushing about, some with injured patients and soldiers, others injured themselves and escorted by Wardens. The PA system fed a constant stream of announcements and pages for assistance. One that repeatedly came up was 'Code White' followed by a location. Wyll and Riis had to take cover multiple times along the way as Berent supporters – most dressed in Stell-Ore security or mining uniforms – opened fire at them. They all fell to Riis' gun.

They were taken by surprise not far from the surgical ward entry. A knot of four enemy soldiers had taken up position in the nurses' station and spotted Wyll before he spotted them. Riis, however, saw them at the last possible second and pushed Wyll out of harm's way, taking a bullet in his left arm. His body armor caught it, but the impact still injured the limb. He returned fire on the four soldiers, taking what little cover there was to be had with Wyll behind an abandoned cart of medical supplies.

Wyll needed a weapon. "Do you have a backup weapon? A pistol, stun grenades – flash-caps? Anything."

Riis gave him a sidelong glance. "You're still in Council custody. I can't give you a weapon."

"Am I supposed to try to catch the bullets being shot at me, then? This is a war; I need to defend myself."

Riis shot another couple rounds at the enemy, then drew a small, concealed pistol from a pouch on his belt. "Take this."

Wyll eyed the tiny thing. "That toy isn't going to help."

"Take it. It's a lot more powerful than it looks."

He took it, found the safety and switched it off. A whining hum emitted from the gun. Curious, he took aim as one of the three remaining soldiers leaned out to fire at them. A red laser dot appeared on the man's chest. He pulled the trigger and a bolt of electricity sprang forward along the line of the laser like a spark of static – or lightning – hitting the man in the chest and crackling across his body. The soldier gave a short, strained groan and toppled over.

"More powerful than it looks is an understatement. What is this thing?"

"Directed-energy weapon called an electrolaser. More affectionately known as Dewey." He flashed a grin. "Don't get too excited, though. It's basically a Taser with a little more kick. That soldier's not dead, only incapacitated."

"Good enough for now." Wyll took out a second soldier, giving Riis the opportunity to take out the final one.

CHAPTER 28 – MERIS

She tore open the door to see the passage full of people. "Help! The Enforcer attacked us!"

A few people came to a halt, staring at her. She threw one hand to point at the anteroom where Wyll and the Warden were still locked in combat as she tried to help Edzard to his feet. A Sindrian Warden with white-blonde hair drew a slim baton out of a pocket in his uniform trousers and approached her with it upraised, his eyes on the injured Warden. She threw her hands up to ward off the blow, but he stopped and looked at her closely.

"Your eyes are dilated. You've still got the serum in you."

"Uh..."

"Who attacked whom?"

"She attacked us. The Minosian Enforcer."

He jerked his head up to peer at the anteroom. "There are no Minosian Enforcers. Get him out of here," he said pointing to Kier before rushing toward the fight.

Other people in the passage fled through one of the doors in each of the walls, no doubt going to raise the alarm. Meris grabbed the arm of an Egalian woman dressed like a clerk of some sort. "If someone was able to get to us, someone could have gotten to my friends in the Infirmary. Can you get help to them? And Warden Kier needs help, too."

She flicked a gaze at the Warden, who was breathing better now but still nursing a very painful throat. He nodded to her and, after a wheezing false start, said, "I'm fine, but she's right, Officer Colphin could be in danger."

"Come with me," she said, leading Meris and Edzard through the door to the right of the one to the waiting room. A guard station stood immediately behind the door and the woman ran up to the counter, startling the female Tudoryan guard on duty. "The witness in the surgical ward may have been tampered with," she said. "We need eyes on him, now!"

The guard Warden brought up the cameras to the ward and cycled through them. Chaos and carnage filled the screens but there was no sign of Zac, his doctor – or Fydach.

The clerk growled in frustration. "Get in there! Find them!"

The Tudoryan guard rushed off through a doorway behind the counter. Meris started forward, but Edzard grabbed her arm. "What do you think you're doing?"

"Helping my friends." She shrugged the Warden's hand off her and jumped up to pull herself onto the counter. She slid across to the other side and jumped down, grabbing an extra baton that was on a shelf under the counter. It was better than nothing, she figured, jerking the door open and rushing along the corridor. He followed just on her heels, as she expected.

Signs set high up on the walls helped her find her way to the surgical wing, passing panicking staff and patients, and Wardens and Enforcers chasing down intruders. At the nurses' station there, they found Fydach kneeling next to the inert body of a Pentarian nurse. He was bleeding from shallow wounds on his face, arms, and chest – and from a nasty-looking 'bolt wound to his left side above his hip. He cocked the arm wielding the baton back when she skidded to a halt before him.

"Wait!" She threw her hands up defensively. Was he secretly a Berent supporter?

"Fyd!"

The Tudoryan Warden's eyes darted toward his comrade, his body relaxing. He stood, putting the baton away. "Ed, glad to see you're still alive. Apologies, Miss Brand. What happened to Lieutenant Meiryg?"

"We left him in good hands. Riis," Edzard explained. "You're bleeding – can you keep going?"

Fydach nodded. "I'm fine. What happened to you? You sound like a lowlands frog."

"He took a baton to the throat defending us against a Berent supporter," she answered for him.

Fydach's eyes widened, a hint of respect in them. "Guess I missed all the excitement." His expression grew troubled. "Ed, there was an attack here, too. I – I failed."

Her stomach twisted into a cold knot. "What are you saying?"

He looked at the floor. "I am deeply sorry, but your Egalian friend was killed by the intruders. Darius Alazar succumbed to whatever he was poisoned with, too, I was told. He was already in the morgue when we landed here earlier. I'm sorry."

"No..." The floor swayed under her feet and Edzard had to steady her to keep her from falling to her knees. Her whole body trembled, and tears sprang to her eyes to fall unchecked. "No, they can't be – this isn't – Without Darius and Zac, we can't – Berent can't win!"

"I'm sorry, Miss Brand. I did what I could, but we were overrun. I lost the surgeon, too."

"You didn't lose them, Fyd," Edzard said gently. "No one expected war to come here, but it has. And in war, there are casualties."

"Casualties?" Meris asked, incredulous. "They weren't soldiers fighting in this war, they were murdered in their beds!" Tears streaked down her face. Her heart hurt, everything inside hurt. She pressed her hand to her abdomen, gulping in a breath. "God please... It's too much – I can't."

Edzard placed his hands on her shoulders. "Easy, Miss Brand-"

"No," she said, shrugging him off and turning to Fydach. "Tell me what happened to Zac."

"One of the group members broke through, killed the surgeon, and got to the operating table. I didn't really see clearly, I was too busy fighting the rest off, but it didn't look like he used a weapon. I don't know what he used, but I heard the flat line a few moments later. Before I could get to him. I finally fought free and was on my way back to you and Lieutenant Meiryg, thinking you would be the next targets."

"The Adjudicators said Darius was injected with something. Could that be what happened? Where's the man who injected him?"

He shook his head. "He was dressed like a doctor. A Riekan, I can tell you that much. He slipped through during the fight. I'm sorry, I don't know where he is. I assumed he was headed your way – you didn't see him on the way here?"

"We weren't attacked, so apparently not," Edzard answered.

"Where is he? Zac?" She started to charge past him toward the ORs, but Fydach stopped her.

"You don't want to go in there," he said, his eyes troubled. "I had to fight my way out. There are... well, it's a battlefield."

"I've seen battlefields plenty this past week." With that, she rushed through the double doors and into the surgical suite.

It didn't take long to find the right operating room. Blood spilled out into the hall in splotches and was splattered on the window of the door. She took a deep breath, said a prayer, and entered the room.

Carnage. Pure carnage met her eyes and assailed her sense of smell. Soldiers, doctors, and nurses lay in heaps all over the room. But it was the sight of Zac's body that rooted her to the spot. He looked... normal. There was no blood other than what had pooled on the operating table from his amputation.

She cautiously approached. His leg was already gone, the wound already closed. He would have been taken to a recovery room only minutes later had they not been attacked. He would have made it. She reached her hand toward his arm and sobbed as her fingers met his cooling flesh.

"I'm so sorry, Zac," she sobbed.

The combined grief and stress of the past week bore down on her all at once. She sank to her knees and cried brokenly. She barely noticed when the door opened and Edzard knelt next to her.

"Miss Brand, you should not stay here."

She wiped her eyes and nose. "Where else should I be? My friends are dead, Wyll is... I don't even know if he's okay, and the Court has been overrun with Berent's soldiers." She sniffled. "All I wanted was justice for Ellias' and his crew's deaths. I just wanted Berent arrested and sentenced for murder. I never wanted this." She gestured at the bodies around her.

Edzard's stoic face softened. "I understand. But we need to get you someplace safer."

A choking, gurgling cough tore her attention away from the Warden and to the bodies lying next to the operating table. The doctor. He was still alive.

She and Edzard rushed to him. The Warden pulled the bodies of the dead off him. Meris knelt and took his hand. "Can you hear me, Doctor? We're going to get you help."

His eyelids slid slowly open. "No," he said, his voice barely audible. "Too late. For me, but maybe not for them."

He pressed a small glass vial into her hand. It didn't look like the other vials she had seen in this hospital or the one out of which they'd broken Darius earlier in the week. This one was brown with a black lid. She lifted the vial into the light, holding it carefully. A handwritten label had been taped onto the glass:

Watershade extract

She gasped, nearly dropping the bottle. Edzard was at her side almost immediately. "What is it?"

"Watershade," she whispered. "We have to find another doctor. Hurry."

She turned on her heels and sprinted down the hallway in the direction she'd last seen a doctor heading – toward the Morgue. The two Wardens rushed after her. The corridors leading to the morgue were lined with Wardens and Enforcers at every intersection. Most were simply standing guard; others were firing down the hallways they guarded. Whenever this was the case, Edzard and Fydach would push her behind them and take cover with her until the skirmish was over. As soon as they got the all clear, however, she would sprint ahead of them again.

"Miss Brand, wait!" Edzard said once again as she neared the door marked 'Morgue.'

"There's no time!" she called back to him over her shoulder as she pushed backwards through the door.

She turned around inside the morgue and froze. It took a moment before the scene before her made sense. Two nurses lay on the floor with blood pooling beneath them. A Riekan man dressed like a doctor knelt next to one and stood, drawing a scalpel out of the nurse's throat as he did so.

"Who-?"

With a motion too quick for her stunned brain to follow, he grabbed her arm and pulled her to him, turning her to face the door as Edzard and Fydach entered. She sucked in a breath as she felt the sharp edge of the scalpel press to her throat.

"Don't come any closer!" the imposter doctor screamed.

The two Wardens froze, shock registered on their faces. The Riekan man pulled her back until they were up against the wall adjacent to the door. "Get back," he ordered as Edzard tried to inch closer. "Stay back or I will kill her."

"Easy, friend," Fydach said. "I just need to know, are you with Alazar or Berent?" He made a gesture toward Edzard and then himself. "My friend and I, we're with Berent ourselves."

Edzard's face betrayed no reaction. Meris, however, was too shocked to keep silent. "I knew it! You lying pieces-"

The Riekan tightened his grip on her. "I don't believe you."

"I can prove it," Fydach said, taking a cautious step forward. "I can show you my orders from Berent himself." He indicated a belt pouch on his right hip and took another step forward.

"Fine, but your friend stays back until I'm certain. Then we can kill her and find that Tudoryan traitor and put an end to this whole thing."

"Exactly," Fydach said, slowly reaching toward the pouch. "Taking out these two are the last loose ends. Here," he said, dipping his hand into the pouch.

The Riekan relaxed his grip on her slightly as his attention was apparently diverted by Fydach. She, too, was riveted on watching his right hand. But when he made a grab at the doctor's arm with his left hand, the Riekan struck out with the scalpel, catching Fydach's forearm and leaving a long, nasty gash before he could disarm him.

"Lies!"

The Riekan waved the scalpel at Edzard, who had moved in while he was distracted. The Sindrian Warden stopped cold and held up his hands. Fydach had fallen back more toward the door and was trying desperately to stop the bleeding to his wound. Meris gasped when the scalpel was once more held to her throat, knowing that he would kill her any second.

"Everyone stay back!" The Riekan yelled. "I have to make sure it's done. I have to finish it and then everything will be over. My son will be avenged and Berent will be free. We'll have everything Alazar was too afraid to take for himself. We'll make Stell-Ore into what it always should have been."

"And what is that?" Edzard asked carefully. "What should Stell-Ore be?"

The Riekan's laugh ruffled her hair. "The most powerful force in the entire Newverse. Bolidium weapons, an army kitted with Bolidium armor. Unstoppable by any other weapons out there."

That's why Berent wanted to take over Stell-Ore. He didn't care about the commercial and industrial uses for Bolidium, he wanted to militarize it exclusively. Of course, why hadn't she seen it until now?

"Stay back!" The Riekan shouted once more as Edzard shifted his posture.

A voice issued over the overhead PA system: "Code White, Morgue, All available, Code White, Morgue."

The Riekan looked up and in that moment of distraction, Edzard made his move. He lunged forward and struck at the imposter doctor, pushing Meris free in the process. The scalpel still managed to slice a gash up part of her neck and cheek as she fell sideways onto her hip. Blood slicked down her skin and she slapped her hand over the wound as she half-crawled, half-dragged herself further away from the two men fighting.

"Over here," Fydach called to her.

She scooted more toward him as the door flew open. It was Wyll. Her heart did a little leap of relief and joy as he rushed in and joined the fight. In seconds, he and Edzard had the doctor on the ground, unarmed and restrained. Then Wyll dropped to his knees in front of her.

"Meris? Are you all right?"

"I'm okay, Wyll. It's not as bad as it could have been." She started to tell him about Zac and Darius, but he put a hand to her cheek above the wound her hand covered.

"Sit still, I'll get a hemostat patch." He left a moment but came back with first aid supplies. "Let me see."

"No, you've got to-"

"You are bleeding. A lot. If you don't want to die, let me see it."

She took her hand away and felt blood stream down her neck. He cleaned and dressed the wound quickly. As soon as he was done, he turned his attention to Fydach.

She grabbed his sleeve. "Wait, Darius and Zac-"

"I know."

"No, you don't understand-"

Again, she was interrupted, this time by the entry of a group of Enforcers and doctors. One went to help Fydach while a second dropped to his knees next to Wyll. "Let's get you up," he told her in a thick Tudoryan accent, making her sit on a rolling stool while he saw to the laceration.

Wyll grabbed the restrained imposter doctor by the front of his shirt and was demanding the man answer for what he had done. The Riekan spat at him, missing his face but hitting the floor at his feet, and said, "I gave them what they deserved. Would've given her what she deserved, too. And you. Anyone who supports that traitorous murderer."

"What we deserve?" She heard raw anger and grief in his voice. Then she heard a thud as his fist connected with the Riekan's face. "You know nothing about-"

"Wyll! Stop!" She waved the doctor away. "There's no time for this now. We have to get him out!"

She pushed the doctors away and went to the body drawers lining the back wall. She pulled one open. An unknown patient lay on the tray. Frantically, she started opening the rest of the drawers until she finally found the one that held Darius.

"Help him," she pleaded with the doctors as Wyll came up next to her.

"Meris, they can't," he told her gently. "Look at him. He's gone."

She turned back to the tray. Darius was completely still. His skin was pale, his lips blue. So like how Ellias had looked the last time she had seen him, in a room just like this one. It looked like Wyll was right.

It looked like she was already too late.

CHAPTER 29 – WYLL

He saw signage for the morgue and kept on the right trail until he reached a set of stainless-steel double doors. His hands and knees trembled as he touched the metal handle. It was cold, just like the Stell-Ore Security Compound autopsy room. The room where he'd been confronted with the bodies of the crew of Cartage 15. The bodies he had put there.

He heard shouts from inside the room and peeked through the window to see a doctor holding Meris as a human shield between himself and Warden Kier, a scalpel to her throat. Cale was on his knees closer to the doors, trying to stop the bleeding of a deep gash in his left forearm. Everyone's attention was riveted on each other, they hadn't seen his approach.

What he wouldn't give for a flash-cap.

He withdrew back against the wall next to the door. He had no weapon other than the Dewey, which he couldn't use with Meris in the way. But he'd been trained to fight with his bare hands long before he ever held a weapon. The only problem was that the doctor was facing the door more than the Wardens were; he would definitely see Wyll first, jeopardizing Meris' life well before he got anywhere near to freeing her.

Then he saw the intercom. He didn't know exactly what a Code White was, but he figured it would get some attention. He pushed the button and got as close to the mouthpiece as possible to quietly announce, "Code White, Morgue. All available, Code White, Morgue."

He wasn't sure he'd done it convincingly enough, but it was worth a shot. He heard a scuffle in the room and peered through the glass to see Meris half-sitting, half-lying on the floor, Kier and the doctor going toe-to-toe. Wyll rushed in and charged the doctor just as he slashed the scalpel at the Warden.

Wyll caught the doctor's wrist in a two-handed block, then twisted it until he heard something snap. The doctor howled in pain and tried to punch him with his other hand. Wyll struck him in the gut with his elbow and followed it up with a back-fist to his face, feeling the Riekan's nose crunch underneath his fist.

Kier swept the doctor's legs out from under him, sending him careening to the floor. He gave Wyll a respectful nod before restraining the doctor – if the man even was one. Wyll went to Meris and knelt in front of her. She had one hand pressed to a wound on her neck and cheek. His insides went cold when he saw all the blood leaking between her fingers.

"Meris? Are you all right?"

"I'm okay, Wyll. It's not as bad as it could have been."

She started to say something else, but he put a hand to her cheek to keep her still and help stanch the blood. "Sit still, I'll get a hemostat patch."

He rummaged through drawers and cabinets, but there was nothing useful for a living patient that he could find. But then he noticed a first aid kit attached to the back wall. There we go. He grabbed it and went back to her.

"Let me see."

"No, you've got to-"

"You are bleeding. A lot. If you don't want to die, let me see it."

She took her hand away and blood streamed out. As quick as he could, he cleaned the wound and applied a hemostat patch. In seconds, the bleeding was stanched and she looked a little less pale and shaky. He passed the kit over to Cale, intending to help him dress the wound on his arm next.

Meris tugged on his sleeve. "Wait, Darius and Zac-"

"I know."

"No, you don't understand-"

Several doctors and Enforcers entered the room, taking in the sight with confusion. But then one Tudoryan doctor saw Meris and rushed to her, pulling her up to sit on a rolling stool while his colleague helped the injured Warden. With her in capable hands now, Wyll turned on the Riekan doctor, grabbing him by the front of his scrubs shirt.

"Look at them," he said, pointing to the dead nurses and his wounded comrades. "What have you done? What have you done?!"

"I gave them what they deserve. Would've given her what she deserved, too. And you. Anyone who supports that traitorous murderer."

"What we deserve?" The satisfied, smug look the Riekan gave him disappeared as Wyll's fist struck his face. "You know nothing about-"

"Wyll! Stop! There's no time for that. We have to get him out."

He turned back to see Meris on her feet, frantically pulling open the body drawers lining the back wall. She finally found the one that held Alazar's body. As Wyll moved to join her, intent on pulling her away from the body, she turned to the doctors and pleaded, "Help him."

Alazar was pale and still, his lips blue-tinged. He had been dead a while. Wyll's heart stuttered in his chest. "Meris, they can't," he said as gently as he could. "Look at him. He's gone." He tried to pull her away.

She stared at Alazar's body a moment, then jerked her arm out of his grasp. "No! He injected Darius and Zac with watershade." She pulled a glass vial out of her pocket. "I got this from the surgeon in Zac's OR. There might still be time."

The doctors rushed forward. Before he could really tell what was happening, the Enforcers had escorted the imposter doctor out of the room, Kier was helping Cale to his feet, and the doctors were loading Alazar's body onto a gurney. A confusion of medical jargon filled the air. One doctor rushed out ahead. As the gurney was wheeled out of the room, Meris gave his arm a squeeze and her face held a hopeful look when he turned to her.

"Come on," she said, tugging on his arm.

Kier and Cale fell into step with them, but he heard Kier tell his comrade, "You need to be seen to properly. Those need stitched up."

"They do, but we're in the middle of a war."

Welcome to your war...

As soon as they stepped out of the morgue, all the lights in the area shut off. They all slowed to a stop and Meris whispered, "What's happening?"

"Stay behind me," Kier told them, easing forward to stand before the gurney and doctor. His eyes searched the gloom for any sign of the enemy, airbolt gun at the ready. After scouting down the next intersection both directions, he gestured for them all to advance with him down the hall to the left.

"How did you know about that... watershade, was it?" he asked Meris.

She nodded, frowning. "It's pretty common where I grew up. We were all warned about it, but it's easy to misidentify. I once knew a boy who mistook it for watercress and ate it. His mother found him – and the plant, thank God – and took him to the hospital. If they hadn't known what he'd eaten, they would have thought he was dead. His heart was beating so slowly, and he was barely breathing. He recovered," she added, but then she shivered. "He told me that he was aware the whole time but couldn't move and was in the worst pain he could have ever imagined. Like every nerve was on fire." A tear slid down her cheek.

Wyll threw a look at Alazar's seemingly lifeless body and frowned. If he and Zac were experiencing the same thing... "They'll be all right, thanks to you." He touched her shoulder reassuringly then dropped back to cover the rear as they continued their rush through the halls.

A rapid staccato of gunfire up ahead made him turn back in time to see Kier duck away from the next intersection, narrowly avoiding the sudden spray of bullets. "Stay down," he whispered to Meris, going up to join the Wardens.

"Six behind the nurses' station," Kier told him. "I took one out, so five left."

"Any way around them?"

Kier shook his head. "Not through these halls. Backtracking would take too long, and I don't know if the way would be clear that way, either."

"The tunnels? What did you call them – the side halls?"

"It's not a direct route and would take longer," Cale said. "The gurney won't make the turns, anyway."

Wyll eyed the still form on the gurney. It had been so long already... they were running out of time to save him. "Then we carry him through. Or find a wheelchair. We can't afford the delay."

"Wyll," Meris whispered, urgency straining her voice.

He held up a finger. "If you take Meris and Alazar to the ER as quick as you can, I'll keep these guys occupied so you don't get followed."

The doctor leaned toward them. "We need to move. Now. He doesn't have long."

Kier and Cale exchanged a look. "Fine," Kier said. "But you get yourself to the ER as soon as you get an opening here." He handed Wyll a pistol. "That Dewey won't cut it this time."

"Keep them safe," he said, accepting the pistol.

"I'm not leaving you behind," Meris said, touching his arm. "Not alone."

"Yes, you are. Alazar and Zac need you and I'll be right behind you." She started to protest, but he cut her off. "Go. Now." He squeezed her hand reassuringly then nudged her back. "Kier."

The Warden laid a hand on her shoulder. "I've got her."

"Thank you."

"Be safe," Meris said, tears in her eyes, as Kier ushered her away, toward a room they had previously passed.

"I'm staying," Cale said.

"No, I need you to keep my friends safe."

"If you die, these guys will just come after them. I can help keep them safest by keeping you alive and taking these guys out."

Kier gave him a grim nod before following the others into the room and closing the door. Wyll scoffed. "I guess that's settled, then."

Cale grinned. "Well, this is our turf and we outrank you, Lieutenant."

"Fine. You ready?"

All mirth evaporated from his eyes. He checked the magazine of his gun. Half full. "Let's go."

Wyll laid down flat on the floor and eased up to the corner, ignoring the twinges of pain along his back. A blind shot of the Dewey straight toward the nurses' station was met with another volley of gunfire. He watched the bullet and bolts hit the corner and the wall opposite the intersection. It was hard to tell the trajectory for sure, but it looked like most of the fire was coming from the end of the station farthest from their position.

He turned to Cale and gestured toward that direction. The Tudoryan Warden nodded and sent a spate of shots toward that area. This was answered by a short scream and more gunfire. Wyll ducked back for a moment, then shot the Dewey again without aiming. He heard a concussive boom as the energy wave blasted off a piece of the station counter. This was followed by a shuffling as paper and other debris rained to the floor.

While the enemy troops were reacting to this distraction, he and Cale both threw a quick peek around the corner. Wyll switched to the pistol and they both fixed on a target and fired.

Cale's went down without a sound from an expertly executed head shot. Wyll's yelped and fell clutching at his throat. Three more to go.

The return fire from the enemy increased in ferocity and soon a large chunk of the wall just above Wyll's head flew off in a shower of tile and stone chips. A piece ricocheted to catch him just above the right eye. He winced but didn't back down. He glanced at Cale, who was waiting for a lull in the fire again. But then, something caught the Warden's attention.

"Back in a second," he said, darting back the way they had come.

Wyll sent a short burst of fire from the pistol toward the enemy soldiers and was rewarded with a grunt and a series of expletives. More bullets sprayed in his general direction. But then Cale was back, with a canister of oxygen. He unscrewed the valve and looked at Wyll.

"If they don't shoot it, we'll have to."

"Do it."

Cale heaved the oxygen tank around the corner. There was a short burst of gunfire interjected by a panicked voice shouting, "Hold your fire!"

Wyll carefully aimed as the canister hit the ground and shot it. The explosion that followed filled the hallway with smoke and debris and made Wyll's only partially-healed ears ring. But there was no more enemy fire.

Coughing, he and Cale peeked around the corner again. The devastation was complete. Bits of the nurses' station mingled with bits of the enemy soldiers. Something inside Wyll went cold and heavy and he had to look away. Cale grabbed him by the shoulder.

"Come on."

But before they got even halfway down the hall past the nurses' station, a short squeal emitted from the PA system. They startled to a stop. "What now?" Cale whispered.

"I see you, Meiryg," an eerily familiar voice said over the speaker.

"It's Berent," Wyll said, dread filling him. "He's been freed. Where are the comms for the PA?"

"All over the Infirmary," Cale answered. "But if he can see us, he has to be in the security suite."

"Don't bother trying to find me," Berent continued. "You may have routed out the cannon fodder, but my loyal elite and I have taken over the brains of this entire building."

In the distance, the sound of electronic locks engaging echoed down the now-silent corridors as if to prove his words. Then, the silence was ruptured by loud, screeching alarms of various sounds and tones all going off at once. The noise was deafening.

Wyll covered his ears. "What are all those?"

Cale leaned in close and shouted. "He's set off every alarm we have. Fire, Code Blue, emergency lockdown... everything!"

A frightened, pain-filled scream eclipsed the alarms before cutting off abruptly. "That was the Sindrian Adjudicator," Berent's voice told them. "This entire planet has been working against me. All of Sindria, that's where I'll begin with my... regime change. Not one single Sindrian will be allowed to live. I'll test all of my Bolidium weapons on this planet before turning them on anyone else in the Newverse who tries to oppose me."

"He's insane," Cale said.

"But first, Wyll Meiryg, you will submit to me. You will come to the Security Suite and turn yourself over to me. If you don't, I will kill the rest of the Council one by one until you do. And if I run out of Adjudicators and Barristers, I'll start on anyone else left alive in this building."

Wyll turned to Cale and nearly shouted to be heard over the din, "Get to the door to the ER department and be ready to run through."

The Tudoryan Warden gave him a worried frown. "What are you going to do?"

In reply, Wyll located the surveillance camera in the hallway and stepped toward it. "Can you hear me, Berent?"

"I can," came the reply.

"I will submit," he said, holding out a hand to stall Cale's protest, "but only if you best me. You let the Warden go. He's injured and needs to get to the ER. He's not part of this, anyway." He held his arms out wide. "This is just between you and me. One on one, hand to hand. No weapons, no backup. What do you say?"

"Lieutenant, what are you doing?"

"Trust me," he said, pulling the Warden over to the ER doors. "Get to the tunnels the second these doors open, I'll keep him distracted."

Berent laughed. "In your condition? You won't last five seconds."

"Then you have nothing to lose." He jabbed a finger toward the camera. "You beat me, you win. I win, well, you'll be dead and won't much care about your grand schemes anymore, now will you?"

"You are a fool, Meiryg. But then, you always were an idealistic simpleton, weren't you? It's a good thing your sister died before she could see you so stupidly throw your life away."

It took all his self-control not to rise to the bait, but the anger, the rage, burned inside. "Yes or no, Berent? If you decline, you'll never find us. Not before it's too late."

There was a long pause. For a moment, Wyll feared Berent was going to go silent and send his 'elite' to gun them down where they stood. But then he heard the PA squeal again, just as he'd hoped.

"Go to the courtyard."

There was a thunk as the doors ahead of him leading toward the East Wing of the Infirmary were unlocked. A second thunk came from the doors to the Emergency Department just behind him. Cale pushed through them, giving him an incredulous shake of his head. But when the doors closed behind the Warden, they thunked locked again. Wyll watched through the doors' full-length glass panel insets, but the second set of doors ahead of Cale didn't open.

Cale tried the handles again, then turned back, a confused frown on his face. Wyll shoved on the doors, but they stayed shut. "Berent! Unlock the doors!"

A red, spinning light went on in the short section of corridor in which Cale was trapped. The Warden jerked his head up, then turned panic-filled eyes to Wyll. "Sterilization protocol!" he shouted.

Wyll turned back to the camera. "Berent! Let him go! This is just between us!"

"Yes, it is, which is why I have no reason to let him live."

Wyll turned back to see Cale throwing himself against the doors opposite. He stopped and took aim at the lock with his pistol. He fired two shots in rapid succession, but when he shoved against the doors again, they remained locked.

A mist sprayed into the corridor. Wyll could hear Cale coughing and yelling over the sound of the alarms. Growls of frustrated panic tore from Wyll's throat as he shoved his shoulder against the doors over and over, to no avail.

Cale came back to the other doors and tried to open them from the inside as Wyll pushed from the outside. Still, they didn't budge. The Warden jerked on the handle one more time then dropped to his knees, choking on the mist. He lifted his head, tears streaming down his face, though Wyll couldn't tell whether from fear or the sting of the mist filling the area.

"No!"

Not again, not another one. Wyll pounded his pistol against the glass, but it would not give. He sank to his knees and laid his left hand flat on the glass. They locked eyes for a long moment, then the Warden gave him the Tudoryan salute – left arm behind the back, a closed right fist over the heart and slight bow of the head. Wyll returned the salute, keeping his eyes locked on the Warden's.

The mist ignited in a flashfire, the intensity of which Wyll could feel through the heavy door and thick glass. Shock and horror rooted him to the spot, and he could only watch as the fire engulfed the Warden. In seconds, the flame winked out, leaving its afterimage seared on Wyll's retinas.

Cale's body was nothing more than a heap of charred remains.

Wyll let out a scream of rage and grief. He jumped up and spun around to face the camera again. "I'm coming for you, Berent! This ends today!"

CHAPTER 30 – WYLL

There were so many ways this could go wrong. Most of them boiled down to Berent's treacherous nature – which he'd once again demonstrated in horrific clarity. But in the back of his mind, Wyll feared he would simply lose. And if he lost, he would die; if he died, Berent would kill Meris and the rest of the Council.

And if the Council fell... all Sindria and then the rest of the Newverse could fall with it.

Other than passing out from pain on the flight to the Council Court from the forest, he hadn't slept in far too long. None of them had had a chance to eat more than a handful since they'd fled Stell-Ore, either. He had nearly lost to that Pentarian in the forest because of pain and fatigue. Berent was right; he was in no shape to win this fight.

But the image of Cale's body was seared into his brain. One more for Berent to account for. One more for Wyll to account for, as well.

The doors to the elevator he'd been led to slid open to let him out. The emergency shutter blocking the intersection to his left rattled as it lifted open. It just as quickly shut again behind him the moment he stepped through. Berent was guiding him to the courtyard – and blocking off his access to any other part of the Court.

At least, he hoped he was being led to the Courtyard and not to an ambush somewhere else. Not to another death trap like Cale. His hand holding the pistol began to shake. With a grimace, he clutched it tighter and began to pray.

Father above, please give me the strength to do what must be done. Please be with me and protect my friends and the members of the Council. Please welcome Warden Cale into your kingdom, Lord God. And if it is Your will that I should die today, too, please forgive me my sins and allow my soul to enter Your eternal embrace. I have done so much wrong, Lord. I didn't know – I thought I was doing the right thing, but now I know I was being used for evil. Please tell me the right way to end this and stop the evil. Please, please show me the way. Amen.

After passing through a few more doorways, he paused at the final door to the Courtyard. He rolled his neck and shoulders while he waited for it to unlock. The stretching of the skin on his back hurt more than he wanted to admit, and far more than he was comfortable with for the fight ahead. The numbing agent was fading fast.

The lock released. Closing his eyes for one moment, he blew out a centering breath. Then, knowing he could delay no longer, he opened the door.

The sun was rising. The sky to the east was a lighter shade of charcoal than the rest of the sky. Stars still winked at him, as if either cheering him on or bidding him farewell. Myranda used to love to watch the stars with him when they were kids. He hoped she was enjoying sights far more beautiful than this in Heaven now. Maybe she would show them to him when he got there. *Please let me still get there...*

There was carnage in the Courtyard itself and the stench of death hung thick in the air. A transporter lay in a smoking heap a few dozen yards from the one Kier and Cale had brought them in on and just to the right of the doorway he'd now exited. The bodies of Wardens, Enforcers, Infirmary personnel and patients lay dotting the whole yard. But so were the bodies of some of Berent's soldiers. It was disturbing to see the Stell-Ore Security uniform and equate it with the enemy after so many years of wearing it himself.

A gun's safety clicked off nearby. He stopped, searching the gloom. Berent slowly came into view out of the shadows of Kier's intact transporter. "That's far enough," he ordered, gun leveled at Wyll.

Wyll held his hands out to his sides, the pistol in one and the Dewey in the other. He dropped the pistol. "Hand to hand, one on one. That was the deal. No more treachery. Drop your weapon, Berent."

The Riekan laughed. "I'm trying to figure out if you're brave or incredibly stupid."

"Yeah," Wyll answered with a grim chuckle, "me too."

Berent tossed the gun to the ground. "At least you're honest. Drop the electrolaser and let's get to it."

Wyll dropped the Dewey. "Did you ever love her?"

Berent paused in the middle of assuming a fighting stance. "Of course I did. I still do."

"That's why you killed her, then, is it?"

"That was her own fault. I was trying to kill Meris Brand, not Myranda." There was a touch of tenderness and sadness as he said her name. "But she made her choice." The tender sadness was gone now, replaced with bitterness. "She chose her side and it cost her life. Just like it's going to cost you yours."

He threw himself at Wyll with a growl, fists flying. The assault was so abrupt and fierce, it was all Wyll could do to block and redirect his momentum. They ended up facing opposite ways from where they started and Berent began to circle him with predatory intensity. Wyll kept him in sight, maintaining a defensive stance as he circled with him. The next attack was as abrupt as the first, but Wyll was ready for it. He blocked the jab to his throat with his forearm and kicked at Berent's right knee.

The kick missed its intended target as Berent dodged, but still connected just above the Riekan's ankle. He growled and punched at Wyll's face, catching him in the same spot the chunk of wall had already sliced. Fresh blood spurted from the cut and he had to wipe it away in order to see. Berent pressed his advantage, striking at Wyll's back with a flat hand.

He fell to one knee with a yell. Berent came in for another strike, but Wyll grabbed the ankle he'd just kicked and yanked the Riekan's foot out from under him. Berent twisted to land on his hands and kicked out with his other foot. Wyll dodged, twisting Berent's ankle further until he screamed.

Injured and enraged, Berent kicked at him again, this time catching him under the jaw with the toe of his boot. Wyll staggered back. He lurched to his feet in time to partially deflect a strike to his solar plexus. The blow ended up hitting a spot just above where the Pentarian had stabbed him a few days ago. He gritted his teeth against the pain and caught Berent's arm, wrenching it in the wrong direction.

Berent howled in pain and rage, barreling Wyll to the ground before the bone in his arm could be broken. Wyll's back slammed onto the grass. The wind whooshed from his lungs and starbursts danced before his eyes as he screamed in agony. His former brother-in-law outweighed him by at least thirty pounds and used that extra weight now to pin him down, his forearm pressed into Wyll's throat. Fighting panic, Wyll grabbed the front of Berent's shirt and pivoted his hips to throw the man off him.

It didn't work.

Berent must have expected the move and had braced his feet firmly in the dirt on either side of Wyll. He grinned and pressed harder. Wyll gasped for air and clawed at Berent's arm. His vision was starting to go red around the edges.

The Riekan's eyes gleamed with victory and he leaned closer to say, "I told you you'd lose. And when you're gone, I'm going to hunt down Meris Brand and everyone else who was stupid enough to help you."

Tears of pain and frustration and fear leaked from his eyes. It couldn't end like this. It couldn't be that Berent was meant to win. Could it? *Please, help me.*

His strength, what little was left, was fading along with his consciousness. But with one desperate effort, he struck the palm of his hand to Berent's nose. The Riekan's head snapped back, throwing off his balance and loosening the pressure on Wyll's throat just long enough that Wyll was now able to throw him off like he had tried to do before.

They were both panting, and their skin was slicked with sweat. Wyll rolled away from the man who used to be family, onto his hands and knees, grimacing against the pain the motion caused his back. He massaged his bruised throat and gasped for air. Berent had recovered enough to be on his knees as well, one hand stemming the flow of blood from his nose.

"Nicely done," he said.

This was far from over. He could see it in Berent's eyes: he was going to drag this out as long as possible, relishing the torture he'd inflict on Wyll before the end. He could also see that Berent knew he'd come to that realization. His smirk was full of amusement, his eyes full of the promise of violence. He rose to his feet and beckoned Wyll to him with his bloody right hand.

"Round two," he said, curling the hand into a fist.

Wyll pushed himself up to stand. But before he straightened fully upright, he lunged forward and rammed his shoulder into Berent's midsection, shoving the man back several feet. The Riekan pounded his fists against Wyll's back, eliciting a pained yelp. Wyll maneuvered his feet to trip his opponent, but Berent managed to keep his grip on the back of Wyll's shirt on the way down, pulling him off his feet as well.

Wyll landed on Berent. Shifting his position, he pinned him down with one knee and pummeled his fists into Berent's face over and over until he heard a snap. Adrenaline and rage masked his senses and couldn't tell if it had been his opponent's bones breaking or his own. A mask of blood coated the Riekan's face, yet he grinned and spat out a couple teeth.

Berent laughed, spraying blood on Wyll's face. "There you go," he said, lifting a hand to pat Wyll on the cheek. "That's how we play this game."

The next pat became a gouging rake of his fingers. Wyll's skin tore, sending blood trickling down to his chin. He punched Berent one more time. Then, screaming all the grief and rage trapped inside, he wrapped his fingers around Berent's throat and squeezed.

Berent wheezed a laugh and clawed at Wyll's hands, but Wyll merely squeezed harder. Showing the first little trace of panic, Berent's face was now scarlet and his dark eyes wide. He clawed at the young Tudoryan's face again, desperately. Wyll moved his head back, his tears and blood falling in equal measure onto the Riekan's face.

Berent struck at each of Wyll's elbows, forcing his arms to buckle. Before Wyll could recover his balance, Berent grabbed him by the back of his head and pulled him forward into a head-butt. More stars filled Wyll's vision as he staggered back away from his opponent.

Berent groaned and coughed, rolling onto his side. The slight wince as he did so reminded Wyll that Berent had taken a gunshot to the upper right arm. He slid forward and jabbed two fingers into the bloody wound.

"Round three," Wyll said, panting.

Berent howled and threw a weak punch at Wyll's head, but it barely grazed him. Wyll backhanded the Riekan and shoved him over onto his back again. Gripping the front of his ripped and bloody Stell-Ore uniform shirt in both hands, Wyll lifted him up to slam his head against the ground twice.

Wyll started to lift him a third time, but Berent hooked one arm around Wyll's waist and dug his fingers into the HEL-gun wound. Wyll screamed and twisted madly, trying to dislodge his hand. Finally tearing free, he scrambled backward away and knelt in the grass, winded and shaking.

"You should... give up... now," Berent wheezed as he levered himself up onto his knees. "You can't keep this up... much longer."

"Neither can you," Wyll answered, gulping in a breath.

Berent chuckled. "I only need to outlast you, don't I?" He rolled his shoulders and popped his neck. Then he rose to his feet and held a hand toward Wyll.

Wyll slapped the hand away and started to get up on his own. Berent laughed and kicked Wyll's legs out from under him before he got all the way up. He fell back to the ground on his stomach with a hard whump. He cried out and lay there trying to catch his breath a few seconds.

"Round four," Berent said from behind him.

And then the Riekan was on him, his knee ground into the small of Wyll's back. He grabbed a handful of Wyll's hair to pull his head backward.

"I'll give you credit, brother," Berent's voice snarled into his ear, hot breath and bloody spit fanning over his skin. "I never expected you to last this long in your condition. It was fun while it lasted, but it's time to put an end to it, don't you think?"

Berent snaked his forearm around Wyll's exposed throat even as he pulled his head back further. Gasping for air, Wyll frantically sought a way out. His hands blindly groped across the ground, but all he felt was grass and dirt.

Just as his vision started going dark again and his neck felt like it would snap, his fingertips brushed against something metal. Desperate, he reached for the object, feeling sharp edges gouge his skin. He wrapped his fingers around the metal object and stabbed it into Berent's hand.

Growling out profanities, the Riekan released him to cradle his injured hand. Wyll rolled over and kicked him away. A piece of wreckage from the ruined transporter stuck out of the back of Berent's hand a few inches. When Berent tried to make another grab at him, he saw that the metal piece had also pierced all the way through his palm. Wyll dodged and kicked out hard one more time, catching the Riekan in the temple.

Berent collapsed in a heap, unconscious. Slowly, Wyll levered himself to sit on his heels, panting with exhaustion and grimacing with pain. He took a moment to just breathe and scanned the ground for his weapons. He spotted his pistol first and made his shaky way over to it and the Dewey several inches further away. A warm trickle on his throat distracted him, and when he touched his fingers to the spot, they came away slicked with blood. He'd come far too close to impaling his own throat with that piece of wreckage.

Pressing his hand to the wound, he picked up the pistol. Behind him, he heard Berent begin to stir himself awake. Wyll closed his eyes a moment before turning to aim the gun at his former brother-in-law's head. His hand shook as he hesitated.

He could do it. Just a squeeze of the trigger and it would be over. All the lives lost would be avenged and all future loss of life would be prevented. He could do it.

But Berent was unconscious and no longer an immediate threat.

But when he woke up... They would be back to square one and everyone on this planet would be in danger. He could prevent that from happening right now. All he had to do was pull the trigger.

After all, Berent Gaehts deserved to die for his crimes.

He did deserve it.

But this was not the way. Wyll would not become a murderer. He would not become like Berent.

Blowing out a shaky breath, he blinked away tears and lowered the gun.

Out of the corner of his eye, he noticed the body of an Enforcer lying a few dozen yards away. Going to the body, he retrieved a pair of plastex handcuffs, which he used to secure Berent's hands behind his back instead. Standing again, he lifted his eyes to the east sky, seeing the first blush of pink and gold rays of sunlight on the horizon. He took a deep breath and simply watched the colors change a few moments.

The door to the Court banged open. He spun toward it, pistol up in a weak but defensive posture. It was Meris. With a grateful sigh, he dropped the gun and took a few weary steps toward her. Behind her came Wardens Kier and Riis. He stopped. Did they know about Cale yet?

"Wyll!" Meris barreled into him, throwing her arms around him. "Thank God you're alive."

He winced but hugged her, too. "Easy," he said a moment later, reaching back and taking one of her hands in his to bring it to the front away from the HEL-gun wound.

"I'm sorry," she said, releasing him. Her eyes scanned his various injuries. "We need to get you to the Infirmary."

"I'll be okay now." He turned his attention to the two Wardens who now joined them. "Kier, I'm sorry but – Cale, he... he didn't make it."

Kier nodded, his eyes full of pain and anger. "I know."

Meris' concerned frowned melted into a joyous smile. "Wyll – Darius and Zac, they're going to be okay."

A chuckle of disbelief and relieved gratitude bubbled up out of him. "Oh, thank you, God!" He clapped a hand to her shoulder. "Come on, I want to see them."

He saw her expression change just a fraction of an instant before she screamed his name in warning and in the same instant an intense but brief piercing pain tore through his lower back.

Time slowed. Kier and Riis shouted and dashed past him. He heard the thumps of a rifle butt thudding into flesh. He turned his head to see Berent, his hands free and with no sign of the piece of wreckage, lying unconscious on the ground, his head and face bloodied.

Meris scrambled to catch him as he sank to his knees before her. She was saying his name, talking to him, but her voice sounded miles away. He frowned in confusion, gripping her arms for support because, somehow, he could no longer hold himself upright on his own. She sank to her knees with him to keep him from falling.

With a jarring snap, time reverted to its normal rhythm.

"Don't try to move." Tears poured down her face. "Can you hear me? Don't move."

"I'm okay," he told her. "It's okay, I just need to get my feet under me again."

Kier and Riis circled back to face him, their expressions shocked. Meris pleaded with them, "Help him! Please!"

Fear coursed through him as his brain started to put together the reality of his current situation. "Meris, what's wrong? I don't feel anything wrong. I don't feel – Why can't I feel it?" He dropped one hand from her shoulder to reach behind him.

"No!" She stopped his arm then took his face between her hands. "Look at me. Don't move. Okay? You have to stay still."

"Why are you crying?" He brought his hand up to wipe away her tears, but his whole body felt clumsy and hard to control. His fingers pressed limply against her cheek. "What's happening...?"

His last reserves of energy depleted, he slowly fell forward into her arms. She clutched him tightly and he started to warn her not to touch the wound on his back, but realized it no longer hurt. Nothing hurt much anymore. He took a breath and felt his whole body go slack against her, his head coming to a rest on her shoulder.

The glorious sunrise met his eyes.

"Do you see it?" he whispered.

A moment later, he felt himself being lifted into the air. Voices spoke urgently all around him, but he couldn't focus on them. No longer able to watch the morning dawning, he sighed and closed his eyes, giving into exhaustion.

CHAPTER 31 – MERIS

She found him in the workshop. Watching him work a moment from the open doorway, she marveled again at how this stranger – and all the others – had come to be so important to her, so much a part of her life, in such a short amount of time. He should have been resting, but, of course, his natural stubbornness won out.

"The curse of Sindrian stick-to-itness," she teased as she entered the workshop.

Darius turned toward her, his eyes lighting up as they always did when they found her. With a smile, he held up the prosthesis he'd been working on, having to use both hands to make up for nearly half of his fingers still being splinted. "It needed to be lighter. He can get around with the other one well enough, but the design was too... clunky." He shook his head. "This one is thirty percent lighter and just as strong, if not stronger."

She smiled. "He'll be grateful."

"I hope so. And I hope he won't be the only one." He sat the prosthesis aside and a glimmer of excitement danced in his eyes as he told her, "I'm expanding Stell-Ore. Yes, we'll still be the Newverse's premier Bolidium mining and refinery company, but I'm opening a medical R&D department. Prosthetics, surgical tools, other medical devices... I want to ensure Bolidium gets used for more than weapons and industry. I want to save lives."

"That's fantastic," she told him, sharing the excitement of the prospect. "But you should start with your own: you should be resting. You were on a morgue slab less than a week ago."

His eyes grew troubled, dark with remembered agony. "I am aware. Believe me."

She stepped forward and lightly touched his hand. "If you want to talk about it, you know I'm here."

He dropped his gaze to the ground and nodded. "Thank you, but I can't place such expectations on you." He moved away just enough that her hand slid off his. "You have your own life to go back to once this is over. You don't need to take care of me. Anymore," he added with a self-deprecating grin.

"Darius... I don't know if I could ever-"

"I know, Meris." He looked up at her with a sadness in his eyes that made her heart ache. "All that needed to be said has been said."

"Not all," she disagreed. "I don't know if I can ever come to care about anyone the way I love Ellias." She touched the dog tags she wore on a chain around her neck with the hand that bore the engagement ring and its matching wedding band. "But if I could, I would care for you. But it's not fair for you to put your life on hold for a maybe someday. You deserve to be happy now, with someone who can be with you now."

"I am happy now. We've been granted our freedom – pardoned with the Council's gratitude and commendations, nonetheless. I have my company back. And I have new friends." He made a gesture back toward the house across the yard from the workshop. "I have my life here back. And it's a good one."

He made a shrug with a tilt of his head. "If maybe someday ever comes along, I would simply be happier."

She looked away. "Should I get Zac?"

"Yes," he said after a moment. "This one is ready. I'm still working on the other one."

"How close are you to getting it adapted, do you think?"

"It will be done today. I'm just having trouble with the bulkiness. And with my hands..." He turned a frown at the other device heaped on the workshop table. "If I can pare down the connectors, it can be worn under clothing. Right now, it still is a bit too... industrial."

"You'll get it. And if not today, the way it is now is still an improvement over the alternative. He'll be grateful either way."

"I hope so." His face held the heaviness of guilt it so often wore these days.

"Hey, keep in mind none of this was ever your fault. All right?"

He sighed and gave her a sad smile. "So you keep telling me."

"Because it's true."

"It isn't yours, either, Meris. You keep forgetting that, as well."

Her lips stretched into a wry half-smile. "It seems we both have things to remember. I'll be right back, okay?"

"All right."

Warm afternoon sunlight washed over her as she exited the workshop again, making her squint against its glare. This place, Darius Alazar's home, wasn't what she expected of the Newverse's top industrialist. The neatly trimmed grass path she took meandered between two meadows of wildflowers and tall grasses and she skimmed her fingers through rows of seed heads nodding in the light breeze as she walked. At the white wooden arbor and the fence that stretched out in either direction from its sides, the meadows ended and a lush but more formal garden took over. Up a manicured hill dotted with roses and other exotics, natural stone steps cut a path leading up to the house. Comfortable and charming in its undersized grandeur, the house was a cross between a stone cottage and a manor house. It was large enough to border on stately, but small enough to border on cozy. A reflection of its owner's dichotomies, in truth.

She loved it immensely.

She entered by the kitchen's rounded-top wooden door, figuring Zac wouldn't be too far from the pantry or fridge. She grinned to see that she was right. He greeted her with a distracted smile from where he stood in front of the sink, rinsing a plate he'd just washed.

"Hey," she said, "he's got the new prototype ready for you to try."

He glanced down at the prosthetic on his leg. "I keep telling him there's nothing wrong with the one the Council doctors gave me." He frowned and put the plate on the drainer. He still didn't like discussing his lost limb, or what had happened to him afterward.

She tucked her arm around his. "Humor him. Please. It's his way of making up for some of it."

"There's nothing for him to make up." He turned off the water and dried his hands on a towel.

"I know that, and you know that. But he feels it. The weight of it, the burden... he carries it. I still do, too. But it helps to know we didn't lose, even if we didn't exactly win. It also helps to know with what's coming tomorrow, it will finally be over."

He placed his hand over hers and leaned his cheek against the top of her head. "I wish Wyll could be there to see it done."

She sighed, a lump forming in her throat. "I know. Me too." She tugged on his arm. "Come on, he really wants you to try this new one."

"Fine," he said, following her out of the house and back to the workshop.

After dinner that evening, as the sun was setting, she took the path back out to the meadow. But this time, instead of going to the workshop, she took a side path to the back of the meadow, gathering a handful of wildflowers on the way. She passed the orchard and stone well, then the greenhouses and continued to the small clearing along the corner of the fence. The plot was simple but nice, like the headstone, which was engraved only with his name and the inscription: *Brave comrade, beloved friend*

Darius had insisted on the grave being here since he'd had no family on Sindria or his home planet and the first thing they had done yesterday was bury him. After that, Darius had gone back to survey the damage at Stell-Ore. He'd told her there was something he needed to find to help make things right. She'd gone with him, there was something she needed to find, as well.

The entire company had come to a screeching halt after the uprising, so the whole place was empty when they arrived. Though the bodies of the dead had been removed by the authorities, their blood remained. Everywhere. At first, he'd stopped at every stain so they could pay their respects, but after a while, it became clear there was virtually no end to the blood that had been shed in those halls and she had pulled him away so they could do what they came to do. And while he was getting what he came for, she had gone to Ellias' quarters.

The moment the door opened, and his scent and the sight of his belongings hit her, she felt the loss of him like it was brand new. Crumbling to her knees, she sat on the floor of his room, weeping as her heart broke all over again. Eventually, however, the tears slowed and the squeezing on her heart eased enough she could stand again.

He hadn't kept many personal items here; the majority of his belongings were at his apartment. But the things he had wanted nearest to him during the long stretches he would spend here, the things he most cherished, that's what she was here for. His body and the remains of his crew members had been removed from the Stell-Ore morgue and, because of convoluted legal proceedings, were still awaiting burial. She wanted to have his effects to give to his mother before the funeral, which, in a turn of profound poetic closure, was going to be the same day as Berent's execution. But she saw one thing immediately that she would keep for herself.

The photograph on the wall next to his low-grav bed pod had been taken only a few months ago. In it, they sat under a fir tree in a patch of swans-bonnets, the little blue flowers like a carpet beneath them. She wore a purple dress and his pale blue lightweight sweater, which was so large on her it swallowed her up, but she had refused to let him compress the fibers to fit her better. Her hair was its original length, down past her shoulders, and her natural honey blonde color, not the above the shoulders brown style she'd adopted when infiltrating Stell-Ore.

She had both her arms wrapped around him, her hands barely visible inside the cuffs of the sweater, and was laughing so hard her eyes were closed. She couldn't remember now exactly what he'd said to make her laugh so hard, but she wished she could. He had made her laugh so many times every day it was hard to keep track.

Ellias wore civilian clothes: a long-sleeved dark blue shirt that complemented his eyes and gray trousers. He was holding the camera, his other arm around her waist, and was kissing her cheek and looking at the camera from the corner of his eye. He was happy and healthy and full of life. He was beautiful.

A few hours after the photo had been taken, he'd asked her to marry him. A few weeks later, he had been killed.

With trembling hands, she took the photograph off the wall and pressed it to her chest. That was the moment she wanted to hold onto and never let go of, not the memory of his distress after watching his crew die. Not witnessing his own life being snuffed out in an instant. Not seeing his body on the autopsy table at Stell-Ore.

Everything else – his clothing, the timepiece his father had left him, his favorite book and music streams, the little tokens and trinkets he'd collected throughout his life – all of that she gathered up on his bed to put in the trunk she'd found in the closet. She heaved the trunk onto the bed and opened it. A little hinged box fell out of an interior pocket and now lay in the very middle of the trunk's bottom.

Frozen, she could only stare at it a long moment before, finally, picking it up and opening it. The rings sat side by side on a cushion the same blue as the Helsing sea at high tide. His grandparents' wedding rings. What would have been their wedding rings.

The white gold bands were plain other than a thin line of braiding down the center. It was a three-strand cord, said to symbolize the intertwining of the bride, groom and God through their marriage. The engagement ring was the same as the wedding rings but also featured a small, square-cut diamond atop a short prong setting. She had seen it when he proposed, and he'd placed it on her left forefinger in the Sindrian custom when she'd accepted, but it didn't fit. His grandmother was a more... robust woman. He'd told her he knew going in that it would need adjusting, but he hadn't wanted to wait for it to be done before asking her to be his wife. So, he'd taken the whole set back here with him, intending to have a jeweler in the area resize it.

She cried when the rings slipped onto her left forefinger like they had always belonged there. He had gotten them resized as promised. No doubt he had tucked them into the trunk for safekeeping until he could bring them home after the stint on Thalassa.

She was still wearing them when Darius had found her a few minutes later. He didn't say a word, merely helping her carry the full trunk to the transporter. Nevertheless, she tried not to call too much attention to them as she opened the cargo hold; his guilt when he had seen them was all too evident in his expression.

Pieces of the prototype mining suit like the one that the Pentarian who had attacked them in the Security compound had been wearing, along with other bits of body armor and some tools, had already been loaded up. She'd scolded him for not waiting for her to help him load the gear, knowing how tenuous his condition still was. He'd smiled and promised to take it easier the rest of the day.

And he had. Technically. Taking the pieces to his room, he'd spent the entire day designing the prostheses he'd been working on this morning.

She used a stem of grass to tie the small bunch of flowers together before kneeling to lay them on the grave. "I figure you already know this, but tomorrow is the day. The Council Court has been reclaimed and things are starting to go back to normal, as far as functionality goes. They're appointing an interim Sindrian Adjudicator to sit in on the proceedings until an official replacement can be named. But tomorrow it is."

She shivered, despite the warmth of the evening. "I thought I'd feel differently about it, you know? But even though I know it's the law – and what I feel he deserves – I just can't feel happy about the fact that Berent Gaehts is going to die tomorrow. He was Ellias' best friend and the husband of my best friend. He was my friend, too. And now all I can wonder is whether it was a lie all along, or if he became this... monster over time, or..."

She picked at a few stray leaves from the bouquet and sighed. "It all seems so stupid and pointless. All those people he killed – Ellias, Myranda... you – what was it even for? To become the owner of a mining company? To build an army and take over the entire Newverse? How did he ever hope to accomplish that, or sustain it if he ever did accomplish it? It just... It doesn't make any sense that he could turn his back on us and everything he said he valued for something so material and evil."

"He was insane," she heard Wyll's voice say. "Nothing he wanted or did made any sense."

She sniffed and looked up at the sky. "I guess I'm just trying to understand why." Somewhere, a night bird called out a plaintive cry. "Why any of it. You know?" she asked, turning to him.

Wyll nodded and moved his wheelchair closer, its thrusters near silent as it hovered over the grass. "I went down that path. But now, I'm just glad we survived – even like this – and want to put it all behind us. I've decided to leave the 'why' to God."

Taking a deep breath, she blew it out slowly and nodded. "I suppose you're right." She got up and dusted off her pants, then touched the top of Leo's headstone in farewell. "I'll give you some time with him."

There was a deep sadness in his eyes. "I've paid my respects. I can't..." He looked away and sniffed. "I actually came looking for you. Alazar thinks it's ready and I... I would like for you to be there."

She smiled and took his hand. "I wouldn't miss it."

He squeezed her hand and led the way back to the house. She could feel him trembling. Her heart ached for him.

In those first few hours after Berent had stabbed him in the back with that piece of metal from the wrecked transporter, none of them expected Wyll to live. Not with the Infirmary in the shape it was in and not with so many of the medical staff killed or fled. But the doctors who had saved Zac and

Darius got him into the only sterile operating room left within minutes of the injury. They removed the metal piece and minimized the damage as much as possible. They saved his life, but not his spine.

By unspoken agreement, she, Zac and Alazar had stayed at the Infirmary even after they'd been officially pardoned while Wyll recovered. They had then spent the days since Wyll was released here at Darius' home. Wyll had been given the news of his paralysis by the Council Court Infirmary doctors just hours after the surgery, days ago now, and had taken it much more stoically than anyone expected. A few nights, however, she and Zac had heard him sobbing in his room after Zac had helped him into bed.

The trembling of his hand now told her he was scared this contraption of Darius' innovation wouldn't work. It would be like getting paralyzed all over again. She prayed it would work the whole way back to the house.

The lights streaming through the windows beckoned them on and she sighed as they topped the hill. "What is it?" Wyll asked.

"This place... I'm going to miss it. Being somewhere that doesn't hold memories of Ellias or the others has made it a little easier to deal with losing them." She frowned. "Or maybe it's just letting me pretend we haven't lost them. Either way, it will be hard going back to the real world."

"The real world..." he mused, slowing to a stop next to her. "That's how I've been thinking of it, too. Although it also sort of feels like going back and facing our new realities will be like falling into a nightmare and this reprieve has been the real world instead."

"Darius said earlier today that I have my own life to go back to once this is over. But I don't even know what that life is anymore. Ellias is gone. Myranda is gone. My parents and I..." she shook her head. "They haven't even tried to contact me once since all this happened and I doubt they will anytime soon."

"I'm sorry," he said sympathetically.

She made a dismissive gesture. "Don't be. They have always been too busy to really pay attention to me; it's nothing new. But I also quit my job before going to Stell-Ore. Did I tell you that?"

He frowned and then scoffed a light chuckle. "You know, I never even once thought about you having a job before all this. What did you do?"

"I was a secretary for a primary school office."

Now he laughed outright. "Okay, yes, I can easily picture that."

"I'm choosing to take that as some sort of compliment." She bumped his arm playfully. "But, yeah, I don't know what I'm going to do now. After everything, the scandal, I highly doubt they'll hire me back. Even if I've been cleared and pardoned."

"Alazar would hire you in a heartbeat, you know."

She sighed again and threw a glance at the house. "Yes, he probably would."

Wyll got quiet for a moment, then asked, "You do know that he's in love with you, don't you?"

She looked away from him. "But he knows how I feel. Ellias... I couldn't..." She caressed the rings on her finger.

"We have a saying on Tudorya: 'Love never dies – but that doesn't mean you can never love more than one person in your life.'"

"I haven't even buried him yet," she said, sharper than she intended. "I'm sorry. It's just we – Sindrians – tend to have a hard time with the emotions that leave us... vulnerable. But I'm not particularly good at hiding them. Not yet."

"Emotions aren't the enemy. Not always."

She smirked. "Well, you would say that. Tudoryans have a romantic streak as wide as the Fornisian Asteroid Belt."

"Not all of us," he replied with an amused curl of his lips. "I'm just saying, you're human, you're allowed to feel. And for the record, Alazar's not particularly good at hiding his feelings, either. Not when it comes to you, anyway. And he's got a good fifteen years on you."

"Fifteen? Really?" She glanced toward the house again.

He shrugged. "Give or take. I don't know his exact age, but you didn't expect a twenty-five-year-old to be the head of one of the most lucrative companies in the Newverse, did you?"

"I never thought about it at all. He seems... ageless, I guess." A thought crossed her mind. "Looking at this place, his home, and what Stell-Ore is, it makes me wonder..."

"Wonder what?"

"What he was like before all of this. Which is the real Darius Alazar? The billionaire industrialist or the humble, live-off-the-earth man reflected here? I don't know anything about what he was like before his world got turned upside down."

"I do. And the answer is very much like he is right now. He's been shaken, gotten the ground collapsed beneath him, but he's still the same man he was before. Who he is and what he's done go hand in hand. Just like you, I'm guessing. Just like all of us, for the most part."

"So, you've always been tough, smart and selfless then?"

He frowned and looked away. "No. I was a completely different person after our parents died. Myranda – she was worried about the path I was taking and got me the job with Stell-Ore. It's Hauher I owe for who I am now, ironically. Before Berent lured him to the dark side, for lack of a better term, Hauher was a tough, brilliant and seemingly moral leader. It was his and Alazar's influence that knocked the angry, bitter brat out of me and made me into a man who thought he could do – and be – something good." He opened the kitchen door.

"That's exactly who you are, Wyll. Hauher's and Berent's betrayals don't change that."

He regarded her silently a long moment before gesturing for her to enter the house first.

CHAPTER 32 – MERIS

They passed through the quaint but spacious kitchen, Wyll's wheelchair touching down to glide across the stone floor on its wheels now, and into the inviting living room with its dark hardwood floor and Minosian rugs. Zac sat in the overstuffed Tudoryan tweed armchair next to the fireplace, his legs propped up on a matching footstool. Darius leaned against the fireplace mantle, staring into the cheery little flames and rubbing the palm of one hand across his abdomen in a slow circle. His incision site had finally healed, but the repeated tearing and healing cycle had left a line of scar tissue that he was often seen to touch whenever deep in thought. He and Zac both looked up at their approach.

"Ah, good," Darius said, giving them a smile. "I was beginning to wonder."

She smiled back. "You've finished it?"

"I have. I believe I have." He wavered a moment, then stepped out of the room and around the corner to the study. A moment later he returned carrying the mining suit prototype from Stell-Ore, the same type of suit that Dusa's brother had worn when he attacked Wyll, Myranda and Meris in the Stell-Ore Security Compound's autopsy room all those days ago. This one had been heavily modified especially for Wyll.

Next to her, nervous energy radiated off Wyll as Darius brought the contraption to him. Zac eased his new prosthetic leg off the footstool and rose to join them. Darius knelt in front of Wyll.

"We'll start with it over your clothing, as you're in mixed company," he said, unfolding the full apparatus on the floor. "But it can be hidden underneath in the future, if you prefer."

Wyll swallowed thickly and nodded, his gaze riveted on the device. Darius placed one part of the prosthesis, which resembled a black metal scale-covered boot, over Wyll's right foot and another one over his left, wrapping the black scale body armor fabric around each leg and securing the straps. From there, the structure was a series of piston-jointed supports that formed an armor-clad frame that overlaid his legs all the way up to above his waist. Darius lifted each of Wyll's legs to wrap the armor fabric around and secure the straps around his calves and thighs, then had him lean forward so he could secure the hip and waist straps. The last part was a rigid back support harness that buckled across his chest.

At first glance, it looked nothing more than a modified version of his Security uniform. After seeing the bulkier version in action as an armored weapon rather than its intended use as a tool for protecting miners while tripling their strength, it was good to see the tech being put to this new purpose. She just prayed it worked as Darius envisioned.

As he made the last adjustments to the straps, Darius explained, "There are gyroscope motion sensors in the belt around your waist and chips along your spine that will receive and interpret nerve impulses. You only have to think about what you want to do, and the exoskeleton will do the rest."

Once he had him fully buckled in, he looked Wyll in the eye. "Now, are you ready to stand?"

Wyll was already panting from the exertion of just getting the contraption on, but he nodded. "I'm ready."

Darius pressed a switch on each side of the apparatus along the waist frame. A quiet hiss issued from the device's joints and Wyll startled as the armor went more rigid. He looked to Darius, eyes wide.

"That just means it's working," Darius assured him. "Now, give me your hands." He held his own out and waited.

Wyll nodded and gave Meris and Zac a nervous look. Gripping Darius' wrists to avoid hurting his broken fingers further, Wyll closed his eyes. As gently as possible, Darius pulled him to his feet, the exoskeleton emitting hushed hisses as the frame repositioned to bear his weight. They stayed frozen a moment to test the contraption's integrity.

"All right, let's try all the way upright," Darius instructed in a near-whisper, as if sharing her own fear that speaking too loudly could make the whole thing go toppling down.

A sheen of sweat had already formed on Wyll's brow, but he straightened his torso to stand at his full height, the black scale body armor fabric rippling along his legs as it responded to his movements and thoughts. After another moment of tense anticipation in which the apparatus did not, in fact, collapse, Wyll opened his eyes. Darius grinned and stepped back, still holding onto Wyll's hands.

"It's working," Wyll said, his eyes tearing up. He made a sound somewhere between a laugh and a sob, then turned to Meris and Zac. "It's working."

Meris already had tears slipping down her cheeks. She reached out to touch Wyll's arm, laughing and crying all at once. Zac clapped Darius on the back with a joyful laugh. But delighted as he seemed, Darius was eyeing the exoskeleton with unease.

"Are you ready for the real test, Wyll?" he asked.

"You mean now? Walking?" He threw Zac a look. "Can I do that myself or do I need someone...?" His voice trailed off with uncertainty.

"Maybe..." Meris began, then pressed her lips together. Maybe she should keep quiet and let him enjoy the moment.

Wyll frowned at her. "Maybe what?" He was shaking and beads of sweat were now tracing their way down his face.

"The doctors said not to overexert yourself for the next week or so," she said cautiously. "Maybe we should wait to try walking?"

The expression in his eyes was equal parts frustration and weariness. He turned to Darius, who looked from Wyll to Meris then Zac. Zac gripped Wyll's forearm. "I think she's right. You don't want to set your progress back, undo the healing you've already done."

Wyll's frown was grave when he nodded. But when he looked back at Darius, he said, "Two steps, then. One for each leg, just to be sure it works."

"Are you certain?"

Wyll nodded. "Tell me what to do."

"All right," Darius said warily. "Think about the motion: the rotation of the hip, the bending of the knee, the lifting of the foot. Lean forward a little – not too far – and slightly twist your core in the opposite direction of whichever leg you want to move, and the motion sensors will signal the frame and joints to react. Twist left to move your right leg, right to move your left leg. Carefully. As Zac said, you don't want to hurt yourself further."

Concentration furrowed Wyll's brow, but with an ungainly jerk, he managed to make his right leg inch forward. Darius gave a triumphant laugh and tugged gently on Wyll's left hand while he tried moving his left leg. It moved forward, causing the framework to hiss, but Wyll overbalanced and nearly fell sideways against Meris.

She reached out to steady him. "That was incredible," she told him with a huge smile. "Really, Wyll. Darius, this is a huge triumph."

Wyll's face darkened. "No. I mean, yes, she's right, but I'm messing it up. I need to do better than that."

"You're not messing up, man," Zac assured him. "Trust me, it takes getting used to these things. I'm still learning how to use mine more naturally. In a few days-"

"No," Wyll snapped. "No, I don't have a few days. I have to be there tomorrow; I have to show him he didn't destroy me. Us."

"Wyll," Meris said incredulously, "the doctors said you need to stay home and rest for at least a few more days before going any further. You must give your body time to adjust so your blood pressure doesn't tank when you change position, like it probably did just now. They didn't even want you out of bed and in the chair so soon." She threw a look at Darius, thinking, *sorry, but you know it's the truth.*

His face was resolute. "I owe it to Myranda to see it done."

Zac touched her arm but addressed Wyll. "You could still do that in the chair, though, couldn't you?" he suggested, despite the warning look that Meris gave him.

There was no masking the disappointment in his eyes. "You're right." A sigh. "But that means I *am* going, no matter what the doctors said. There's no discussion on that."

She turned to Zac and Darius. Outnumbered. "Then you should get some rest."

Returning to the Council Court woke the knot in her stomach that felt like it would never go away. All signs of the war waged in the surrounding streets and in its halls had been scrubbed from existence, as if it had never happened. But in her mind's eye, she still saw the bodies and the devastation, heard the screams and gunfire, smelled the blood and smoke.

They were met at their PTV by Warden Riis. His face was more somber than they'd ever seen it but still friendly as he greeted them and led them inside. This time, they entered from the main public entrance, going through a security checkpoint.

Once they were through and met by a pair of Enforcers she didn't know, Riis said, "I will see you all after it's done to escort you out. But now there are more arriving." He gave Darius and Zac a nod, an almost smile to Meris and a respectful bow of his head to Wyll.

The Enforcers led them to the same carraigstone hall with the historical scenes, coming to it from a completely different route than before. Instead of being led to the Court itself this time, however, they were taken to a lower level beneath even the Infirmary. The door of their elevator slid open to reveal a plain stone hallway. It was small, utilitarian, and claustrophobic.

Zac tilted his head toward her and whispered. "I can't imagine walking this hallway knowing the Chamber waited for me. It feels so... hopeless in here."

She shook her head with a slight shudder. "Me, neither." But that's what Berent was about to do, though going by a different route. The thought made her heart ache.

Help me, Lord, not to harbor hate for him. I wish I could simply remember him as the friend he once was to Ellias and to me, as the man who introduced me to my dear friend Myranda. I want to stop the memories there and pretend the rest never happened. But I can't. So instead I ask for the strength to forgive him and then to move on with my life. I ask that for the others, too, Lord God. Let us all move forward and heal.

They arrived at the Viewing Room and the Enforcers left them to seat themselves. A section of seating at the very front was roped off, so she started to lead them to the next row. But a voice behind them said, "Your places have been saved up here."

The Warden who stood behind them was Edzard Kier. She felt herself smiling as she went back up the aisle toward him. He returned her smile and extended a hand, which she shook warmly.

"Warden, it's good to see you."

"And you, Miss Brand." He turned to the others and nodded, extending his hand to each of them in turn. "It's good to see you all. As I said," he held back the roping and gestured toward the front row seats, "these have been reserved for you. Unless you'd prefer further back."

She looked to the others. Zac and Darius looked to Wyll. "Will he be able to see us?" Wyll asked.

Edzard nodded. "He will."

Wyll turned his chair toward the large viewing window, which had its white crystallized privacy setting activated for the time being. After a moment, he nodded to Edzard and moved his wheelchair to the empty space between two of the seats.

"Thank you," Meris said to Edzard. "Will you and Riis join us?"

There was a flicker of smoldering anger that was there one second and gone the next. "If we weren't on duty for the proceedings, we definitely would join you up here. But Riis will be on guard by the door and I will be stationed in the back of the room if you need us. Riis is bringing in the rest of the observers now."

"He mentioned others earlier," Zac said. "Who else will be coming?"

"Several family members and friends of the casualties at Stell-Ore and here have requested to be present as well."

"Has there been any decision made about the supporters who survived?" Darius asked, his expression troubled.

"The Riekan doctor has been found guilty of two counts of attempted murder and multiple counts of first-degree murder of Infirmary personnel. His execution date is still pending. The Minosian woman who impersonated an Enforcer will be facing various somewhat lesser charges and will most likely face life internment. Most of the others are facing similar fates."

His dark blonde eyebrows drew down in a frown. "A small number of your own supporters are also facing charges, I'm sorry to say. Some have been identified as instigators in the riots-turned-war in the streets around the Court, causing the deaths of civilians and Court personnel."

"And I will publicly announce that I never condoned, sanctioned or ordered that," Darius said firmly. "But of those who were detained during or after the fight inside the Court, if any of them are still facing charges, I want to be kept apprised of it. If their actions were justifiable, I want to make sure they receive the best representation possible. Not those Court-appointed Barristers," he grumbled. "No offense."

"None taken," Edzard said with a smile. "Of course, Mister Alazar; I will make sure your request is known." He held a hand toward the seats again. "It won't be long now, if you'd like to get seated."

Zac let her and Darius in first and they took the seats on either side of Wyll. Zac sat next to Meris. Edzard put the roping back in place and stepped back as more people entered the room. Two of these people – a Sindrian man and woman who appeared to be in their early fifties – came over to Wyll and spoke to him in low voices.

The woman held his hand, and Meris, who was trying not to listen in but nonetheless couldn't help but overhear most of what was said, surmised these were the parents of Wyll's best friend, Amund Halsin, one of Berent's first victims.

By the time they left, Wyll had tears trailing down his face. He wiped them away after a moment. A few other people trickled in and Edzard and Riis got them all seated before shutting the door and taking up their positions. The knot in Meris' stomach expanded and twisted as they waited. Then the lights overhead dimmed. Zac took her hand on one side, she took Wyll's on the other. Darius gripped Wyll's other arm.

The glass of the viewing window turned clear. Meris took a shuddering breath upon seeing the empty chair in the middle of a room about half the size of the room they now sat in. The walls were stainless steel, as were the floor and ceiling. The chair, which was bolted to the floor, was padded on every surface with a shiny black material and had thick metal straps on the arms and legs. A large metal container was affixed to the back of the chair. A metal door punctuated the rear wall. A single, bright light over the chair cast a dark shadow on the floor.

Everyone in the viewing room went quiet.

The door of the Chamber opened, letting in a bit more light. A figure clad in a black, masked hood and black robe over body armor – she couldn't tell if it was a man or a woman – entered the Chamber. She could only presume this was the Executioner. Next came the Interim Sindrian Adjudicator. After him was a Tudoryan Warden and a Pentarian Enforcer. Between them-

Wyll's hand squeezed hers in a bone-crushing grip as Berent Gaehts came into view. He wore a plain, close-fitting gray jumpsuit with attached gloves and boots, much like the sealed one-piece suits starship crews wore while traveling between the colony-planets. Shackles weighed heavily on his hands and ankles. Stubble dotted his square jaw; his eyes burned with anger.

And then he looked at the crowd gathered to watch him die and that anger doubled. When he saw Wyll, Darius, Meris and Zac front and center, it tripled. He lunged toward the viewing window, but the Warden and Enforcer hauled him back. He elbowed them both away and rushed to the window, snarling out profanity and threats.

Calmly, Wyll let go of her hand and pushed himself to his feet, faint hissing issuing from the exoskeleton he had apparently put on under his clothes. Meris stood with him, noting that Darius and Zac joined them. They joined hands again. She stared him down as calmly as she could muster, neither triumphant nor grieving. She was determined to give him nothing more than he had already taken.

Berent stopped pounding at the window and stared, eyes hard and cold.

The Warden and Enforcer dragged Berent back and pushed him to sit in the chair. They held him down and secured his arms and legs with the straps. The Adjudicator came to stand before the viewing window. He turned his attention to Wyll and the others, and they took this as their cue to take their seats again. Once she and the others were certain Wyll was comfortably seated – and chided for disobeying doctor's orders – the Adjudicator lifted his hands toward the crowd.

"All gathered here are to bear witness to the lawful execution of Berent Adrik Gaehts." His voice came to them amplified by speakers in the viewing room. "This prisoner has been found guilty of multiple counts of murder and attempted murder, corporate espionage and sabotage, sedition, assassination and acts of war. This prisoner has been sentenced to the Chamber and will be subjected to fatal nitrogen exposure."

A ripple of murmurs spread through the crowd. Beside her, Wyll stiffened as he clenched his fists and jaw. Nitrogen. The Endless Sleep. Berent Gaehts had murdered an Adjudicator and they were giving him the painless death.

Part of her railed at the injustice. Part of her remembered he was still a human being and deserved the same rights as everyone else. Plus, would God want her to wish agony on another person? She took a deep breath and let it out in one quick exhale, taking Wyll's hand. He looked at her and she whispered, "His eternity is in God's hands. God requires justice and mercy from us here in this life. They did the right thing."

The fire in his eyes was slow to fade, but it did eventually diminish. He nodded and turned his attention back to the window. The Adjudicator now turned to address Berent.

"Do you have any last words?"

Berent snarled and spat at the man but, behind his bluster, Meris could see the fear in his eyes. Before she could think twice about it, she raised her voice to him, "It isn't too late, Berent, Not until the last breath. Save your soul, even if you can't save your life. You can be forgiven. God will forgive you. I-" she hesitated. "I choose to forgive you. Please, Berent, make peace with God before it's too late."

For a moment, no one moved or spoke. All eyes were on Berent. His face betrayed nothing of what he felt or thought, but she prayed she had gotten through to him. But then he made a gesture to the Adjudicator, turning hard eyes on the man until he leaned toward the chair. "Release my ashes into the void," he instructed before turning his angry gaze back to her and adding, "where my soul, no doubt, will also be."

Her heart broke. Wyll and Zac both took her hands. Darius slipped his arm behind Wyll to touch her shoulder. She had tried, they all seemed to tell her, and that was all that could be asked of her. She couldn't choose salvation and an eternity of life for him, and he had rejected it for himself.

"Very well," the Adjudicator said. "Have you anything else to say?"

Berent shook his head, keeping his eyes locked on Meris and the others. The Adjudicator stepped away and said, "We shall commence."

The Executioner lifted the hinged lid of the container and removed a clear glass helmet, like those worn while in space as well, that was connected to an interior canister by a long clear tube. He placed the helmet over Berent's head and connected it to the suit. Though his expression did not alter, Berent's breathing became more rapid, fogging the inside of the helmet. He clenched his fists tightly and pulled against his restraints.

The Executioner nodded to the Adjudicator, who in turn gestured for the Warden and Enforcer to join him at the back of the room. Once they were clear, the Executioner flicked a few buttons and switches on the unseen panel inside the container. Berent's vital signs were displayed on a projection in the air above the chair. His heart rate, blood pressure and respirations were all elevated.

Another switch was toggled, and a slight hiss could be heard as the nitrogen began to pump through the tube into the helmet. At first, Berent's vitals spiked to an all new high, but after a few breaths, his pulse began to normalize. He struggled with his bonds and tried to hold his breath for as long as he could, but then, with a raging snarl, he began taking in huge lungfuls of the gas as if desperate to bring on the end.

Several seconds later, he began to shake his head. He appeared to be having trouble keeping his eyes focused on Meris and the others. Eventually, his head fell backward, cradled by the helmet against the back of the chair. He made a sound like a drawn-out, manic laugh that made Meris go cold inside and brought tears to her eyes. His heart rate, blood pressure and respirations began to bottom out.

Thirty seconds became forty-five became sixty... At the ninety second mark, the vitals monitor registered all zeros and emitted an alert that made Meris startle and gasp. The Executioner allowed the alert to continue its long, singular tone for several seconds, then flicked the switch, cutting it off.

Silence fell.

The Executioner pulled out a handheld diagnostic tool and scanned Berent's body with it to confirm he was, indeed, dead. A nod to the Adjudicator then and he began flipping the other switches. When the last had been turned off, he waited a few seconds before removing the helmet and replacing it inside the container. The Executioner then stepped back, and the Adjudicator stepped forward again.

"Let the record show that Berent Adrik Gaehts has died by fatal nitrogen inhalation at two minutes, thirty seconds past the noon hour. The Council thanks you all for your witness. You are now free to go."

Meris blew her breath out in a dry sob. It was over. Berent Gaehts was dead.

Other people in the rows behind them shuffled out of the room, escorted by Riis or Edzard. But she and the others stayed as if rooted to the spot. She didn't understand what she was feeling – or, rather, not feeling.

She finally shook her head and released her friends' hands to dry her eyes. Inside the Chamber, the Warden and Enforcer were bringing in a gurney to remove Berent's body. She noticed the Tudoryan Warden make a quick motion with something shiny at the base of Berent's skull before lifting the body out of the chair. She frowned and leaned forward.

"A precaution, given recent events."

She looked up to see Edzard holding a hand toward the Enforcer and Warden in acknowledgement. The Warden gave a grim nod before wheeling the gurney out of the Chamber. "I don't understand," she said to Edzard.

"Not protocol, and no doubt frowned upon at best and punishable at worst. But necessary, I believed." The Chamber door closed. He gave them a cheerless smile. "A small Bolidium blade inserted between the first and second vertebrae and angled sharply upward. Insurance against any plot to use watershade or something similar to fake heart-death only to smuggle the body out to be revived. Fortunately, Warden Arkwright was thinking along the same lines and was amenable to my suggestion."

She shivered. "Thorough."

"A lesson learned," he said, his eyes flicking from Zac to Darius. He unhooked the rope sectioning off their seats. "Come, I will escort you out."

Wyll remained staring at the now empty Chamber for a moment after she and the others left their seats. Darius gave her a look and she went back to touch Wyll's shoulder. "Wyll?"

"I thought... I thought it would feel different." He closed his eyes and sighed. "I don't feel anything, and I don't mean..." he made a vague gesture toward his legs, then looked up at her. "I don't feel *anything*."

"It's okay. Or at least it will be," she said, squeezing his shoulder in reassurance. "Let's go home."

Home... She meant Darius' house. But it was true, over the last several days, his house out in the countryside had come to feel like home. Wyll, Zac and Darius had come to feel like home.

But now the war was over. Berent was dead. It was time for them all to go back to their own lives. Back to the real world. What would that look like now, after everything? What would they do now? What would *she* do now?

She could see questions like these were going through the minds of the others as they followed Edzard out of the viewing room and back to the main floor of the Court. Riis joined them as they headed toward the exit and the two Wardens saw them safely to their transporter. There was a moment when no one seemed to know what to say, but then Riis gave them a formal Sindrian salute – placing his right palm flat against his chest – and said, "I wish you all well. But I hope to God we don't see any of you here ever again."

"No offense," Edzard added dryly.

Meris smiled at him and Riis. "I think the feeling is understood and shared, Warden. Take care of yourselves."

Edzard nodded. "And you as well, my friends."

They all shook hands and then Zac piloted them away from the Court. Soon the colossal building was nothing more than a miniature, far below. Meris turned away from the view of the

Court and instead turned her attention to the horizon, eager to put the Council and all associated memories behind her.

But there were a few things left to do before she could begin to move on.

CHAPTER 33 – MERIS

"I couldn't face it," Ellias' mother, Tiril, told her when she arrived at the gravesite. "I didn't want the face of the man who took my son from me to be in my mind today. Not today, not while I say goodbye to my baby." Tears streamed from her eyes. Eyes that were so like her son's.

Meris hugged her as tears fell from her own eyes. "I'm so sorry this happened, Tiril."

She patted Meris' back. "Oh, my girl, you have nothing to be sorry for. You are the one who gave him justice."

"I had some help," she said, stepping back to look to Darius, Zac and Wyll waiting nearby.

"Yes," Tiril Gammett said, releasing Meris' hands and turning to the others. "I am eternally grateful to you all." She hugged each of them in turn. "Now," she said, taking Meris' hand again, "I need to put my boy to rest." Her thumb brushed the rings on Meris' finger.

"Is – is that okay?" Meris whispered.

"Oh, yes, dear." She smiled at her. "But don't remain a widow forever. He wouldn't want that for you." With that, she turned away and trudged up the hill where her son's body waited.

Zac pulled her into a sideways hug. "Are you ready?"

"No. But I can't put it off any longer. It's over now, I need to say goodbye." She smoothed the front of her dress – the purple one she had worn the day he proposed.

"We're right here with you," Wyll told her.

She gave him a grateful smile. They had gone through Myranda's wake before this. He would be leaving right after Ellias' service to accompany her body back to Tudorya, again against doctor's orders, where his family would hold her burial. Zac would be taking Jenna back to Egalia after this as well. She would be saying goodbye to them, too, not knowing if she would ever see them again.

Darius, who had been quiet since the execution, gave her a nod and smile. She hated seeing the sadness in it, the guilt and regret it conveyed, but was grateful for his presence. He followed behind as the other two escorted her up the hill to join Tiril.

Each step took everything she had to complete, but eventually she was at Ellias' side. He lay on a floating platform above an open grave. He had been dressed simply, in clothing he would wear to be comfortable, not his uniform or anything formal. Ellias was not a formalwear kind of man. She smiled.

His body had been kept deep-cooled since he'd been removed from Stell-Ore and the damage done to his face from the exit wound had been repaired. He still didn't look the same as he had in life, of course, but it was far better than when she had seen him in the autopsy room at Stell-Ore. She placed a shaky hand on his still, cold chest.

"Goodbye, my love."

Wyll hung back. He had approached the grave with her but hadn't stayed. Meris couldn't imagine how he must still feel.

She turned away and knelt by his wheelchair. "Thank you," she told him.

His brows furrowed over troubled eyes. "For what?"

"You didn't let him suffer. I never told you how much of a blessing that has been for me to know. And for everything you've done since... I am so thankful for all of it. I'm thankful for you, Wyll."

His lips trembled. "I-" He had to stop to clear his throat. "I'm thankful for you, too, Meris. If you hadn't forgiven me, I don't know if I would have been able to see this through."

The clergyman came to deliver the funeral sermon then, and Meris took her place next to Tiril. It was a simple message of the hope of eternity and that Ellias was now free of the shackles of mortality and living on in that eternity. Once his words were spoken, the attendants lowered the platform onto the bed of sweetwood that filled the shallow grave. Large stones lined the perimeter of the plot. A much larger stone stood at the top end, bearing Ellias' name and the date range of his short but wonderful life. Beneath this information was a blessing taken from an ancient Earth song of worship:

Breathe on me, breath of God,

So shall I never die,

But live with Thee the perfect life

Of Thine eternity

Next to the grave, a flame burned in a metal brazier. Branches of sweetwood had been added to the flame and now the attendants gave one to each of them. First Tiril, then Meris knelt and dropped the burning branch of fragrant wood into the grave. Then Wyll, Zac and Darius added theirs.

They stepped back as the flames enveloped the remains of Ellias Gammett.

She watched the flames through eyes blurred by tears. The branches at the outer edge of the pile mercifully blocked her view of its effect. The whole pyre slowly collapsed in on itself, feeding the flames and burying Ellias in one process.

Meris then took his dog tags from around her neck and held them out to his mother, slipping off what would have been his wedding band first. "These helped me feel close to him all through this. I think he would want you to have them now, to help you feel close to him while you grieve. And this belongs to you, as well," she said, offering the ring, too.

Tiril accepted the necklace, but simply took one tag off and threaded the ring back onto the chain. She then handed the chain – with his ring and one dog tag on it – back to her. "We can both feel close to him, and each other, this way."

"Thank you," Meris said through tears. She put the chain back around her neck.

With the comforting rites of burial done, there was nothing left to say or do. Tiril said her goodbyes and the four of them took their leave of each other with promises to meet at the shuttleport in two hours. Everything was happening quickly now. The end was coming fast. She would have more goodbyes to say.

"I hate goodbyes," she said.

The four of them stood in the Interplanetary Departures lobby of the shuttleport. It was a tall, glass-domed space with floor tiles made of Sindrian rose-stone – a slate-like stone with a muted grayish-pink hue – and curved walls of copper and glass. Native trees called ormlauf grew in large aggregate pots, their elegant limbs and serpent-like leaves reaching toward the light above. The place was alive with activity as people on foot and in transporter, PTVs or Darters came and went. Wyll and Zac both had their transporters – gifts from Darius – packed and ready and it was now a matter of waiting for their jump windows to be announced.

"It isn't really goodbye, Meris," Zac said. "I'm coming right back next week. We're both coming back. Right, Wyll?"

Wyll flicked a look at Darius before answering. "Most likely."

Zac frowned. "Most likely?"

"I still have a lot of healing to do. But when the time comes, you lot will be the first to know I'm back."

Her heart sank. "Promise you'll phone or buzz in the meantime?"

A ghost of a smile. "Of course."

Tears were threatening again. She should have been a dried-up husk from all the crying she had done the last few weeks. Her voice thick with emotion, she said, "I'm going to miss you both so much."

"Aww, hon," Zac said with a sympathetic pout. He pulled her in for a hug. "I'm going to miss you, too." He released her and looked at the other two. "All of you."

"You have a place waiting for you at Stell-Ore, if you want it," Darius said, shaking Zac's hand. "Commander Colphin," he added with a grin.

"Commander?" Zac shot a quick look at Wyll.

"I need someone to replace Hauher," Darius replied.

"But, the Lieutenant-"

"It was my suggestion, actually," Wyll said. "Though the thought had already entered his mind."

"I don't know what to say."

"Say you accept," Wyll prompted with a smile.

Zac, who had not released Darius' hand yet, shook it again. "I accept. Thank you, sir."

"Glad to hear it," Darius said, smiling.

A loudspeaker overhead made a short single-note tone. Then a man's voice announced:

<Boarding for the starship to Tudorya has now begun. All passengers report to Gate Twelve and confirm with attendants your vehicle has been docked. Jump initiation in thirty minutes.>

"That's me," Wyll said.

"My offer to you will stand until you are ready to accept it," Darius told him. "Should you so choose."

"I promise to consider it, sir. And thank you." He shook Darius' hand.

"Thank you, Lieutenant Meiryg. Wyll. I owe you, Zac and Meris my life." Darius faced each of them in turn, placing the palm of his right hand on his chest and bowing from the waist. "As one in blood, one in bond ever shall I be."

The Sindrian pledge of fealty, a solemn promise not given lightly. Touched, Meris returned the oath in kind, to him and to the others. "As one in blood, one in bond ever shall I be."

Wyll made the Tudoryan version of the gesture, a fist over his heart and a bow of the head. "By my faith, by my blood, an oath of fealty unbroken I pledge."

Zac, who looked close to tears, brought his heels together and brought his right hand, flat, to touch his fingertips just above his right eyebrow in a salute then brought the flat hand to place above his heart. "My allegiance I pledge, undying and unyielding, to the end of my days."

Then he pulled Wyll into a hug. "Take care of yourself, Wyll."

"You too, Commander."

Zac laughed and released him. "I could get used to hearing that."

Wyll clapped him on the arm. "Be well and safe, and may God shine His mercies on you all."

"And on you," Meris replied, hugging him.

The loudspeaker emitted its tone again. This time, it was a woman's voice that announced:

<Boarding for the starship to Egalia has now begun. All passengers report to Gate Ten and confirm with attendants your vehicle has been docked. Jump initiation in thirty minutes.>

Zac sighed. "Looks like I get to accompany you part of the way now, Wyll. Which is kinda awkward after all that heartfelt goodbying."

Wyll laughed. "That's all right, Tudoryans are quite adept at awkward propriety. And since Egalians don't care much for doing things properly anyway, I think we'll get through just fine."

"Oh, I see. So that's how it's going to be," Zac laughed. He hugged Meris and shook Darius' hand. He then stepped back and told them, "How about we go with 'I'll see you soon' instead?"

Darius grinned. "See you soon."

Meris nodded, still fighting tears. "See you soon. Both of you."

The two of them left then, Zac turning back once to wave from halfway down the concourse. But soon they were both lost to sight among the crowd and by the turning of the hallways. And yet, she and Darius stood staring after them.

"Do you want to stay and watch the jumps?"

"I was hoping you'd ask," she said. "I feel silly, but it's like I wouldn't know for sure they were going to be okay unless I see them go."

He smiled. "I've always felt the same. Ever since I was a boy."

With that settled, they moved to the large windows overlooking the shuttlepads. The Interplanetary ships, Jumpers as they were commonly called, were easy to spot. Nearly three times the size of the domestic passenger ships called Skippers and over five times the size of the city transport shuttles called Hoppers, the Jumpers were like ungainly mother hens, gathering a brood of transport vehicles beneath their sheltering downward curving wings. In between the two wings of docking stations sat the main hub where passengers could sleep, eat and socialize over the course of the journey. A structure attached to the body by a long tail house the complex sublight thrust drives plus all the necessary shielding and whatever else was needed to propel these hens through the cosmos at one-third the speed of sound.

Ellias had once explained the physics behind how it all worked – the cartage crews used starships of similar, though much smaller, design to get to the mining planets – but only the basics had stuck with her. She'd only been off-world once, when she visited Egalia when she was nine, on the only vacation she can remember her family ever taking together. It was fascinating, sure, but it was one of those things she didn't feel the need to understand completely. She knew enough to trust that her friends would arrive at their destinations safely. Wyll would reach Tudorya in a little under three days, with Zac landing on Egalia just under five and a half.

"It always looks like the whole thing should tip forward and stick its skimpy little tail up in the air," she said to Darius as the Jumper to Tudorya was signaled clear for ascent.

"They are... inelegant things, aren't they?" He frowned. "Not at all what I would have designed."

"Really? How would you have them look?"

He smiled a bit self-consciously and looked at the ground. "Oh, I don't know. This design is very practical, certainly. But it lacks... imagination. Obviously, there's no need for sleek, aerodynamic lines in the vacuum of space, but I would love to see something with a bit more style and dignity. Jumpers are too oddly shaped and ugly. But when you barely change the look from the original Earthborns' designs in over seventy years, what can you expect?"

"I guess they thought if it was good enough to get the first colonists here from Earth, it's good enough to get us from one colony-planet to another."

"Yes, I suspect you're right. Is it just me or does that seem lazy and uninspired to you?"

She chuckled. "I never thought about it before, but yes, it does. But if this was the ultimate goal, getting here and expanding our universe this far, maybe they thought there was no need to keep reinventing the wheel, to borrow the old phrase."

He scoffed derisively. But before they could discuss it further, the hydrogen thrusters beneath the Tudorya-bound Jumper engaged, lifting the behemoth off its launchpad to rise rapidly through the air. "There it goes," Darius said, lifting a hand to place on the glass. A telescopic view of the Jumper was displayed next to his hand.

Before long, the Jumper was a mere speck in the stratosphere, even with the telescopic viewer. Then the sublight thrusters took over, slinging the starship hurtling through the void, far beyond their viewer's reach. "God be with you," she said.

Moments later, Zac's Jumper departed as well. Meris lowered her hand from the glass and the viewer closed. "Well," she said with an awkward grin, "that's that, I suppose."

"Yes." His gaze roamed from her to every part of the viewing rotunda before making its way back to her. "Shall I walk you to your transporter?"

At her nod, he fell into step with her back through to the departure lounge. "I'll return the transporter once I'm settled in back at home," she told him.

"Keep it, please," he replied. "The one you came to Stell-Ore in that day was damaged beyond repair during the fighting." He caught her frowning. "Consider it a long-term loan until you get one of your own choosing. Or better yet, consider it your company vehicle. If you were to come work with me, that is."

As Wyll predicted. "Darius, I... I appreciate the offer, but I'm not sure working for you is such a good idea. I don't know anything about mining and my office experience doesn't come close to the level you would need me to have. It's just..." She shook her head.

He had waited her out, but then said, "With me, Miss Brand. Not for me."

They were through the lounge now and approaching the exit to the parking lot. "I don't understand."

"I want you to help me run Stell-Ore. Full partner."

She stopped cold in the middle of the entryway. "Partner? Me? I just got done saying I'm not qualified to even work in your business office, and you want me to help you run the entire company?"

"I do. You are insightful, and your moral compass is unwaveringly aligned. With your help, no one would ever be able to pull off what Berent Gaehts did again. And, if Wyll accepts the position I offered him, you could work with him to help Zac make sure the soldiers are trained ethically and are properly sanctioned."

"Darius, I don't think-"

"This has nothing to do with how I feel about you." He paused a moment. "I don't trust anyone else but you three. Not anymore. Just say you'll think about it. Please."

"I will think about it. I promise."

"All right. Good. Thank you."

They resumed walking out of the shuttleport. It was late afternoon by then, and the sun was moving quickly toward evening. But for now, its light was a wash of warm gold across everything it touched. "Ellias used to say that sunlight like this was as close to magic as we would see this side of Heaven," she said as they reached her transporter. "God's kind of magic, you know?"

He smiled. "Yes. I remember he told me that, too, once. He was talking about you and how he loved to see you in this kind of light. He said, 'It's the only time she's as bright on the outside as she is inside.'"

The tears fell before she could stop them. "He said that?"

"He did."

She laughed through her tears. "I once told Myranda the very same thing about him. The exact same thing. Isn't that funny?" She smiled as tears poured down her face.

"I don't doubt that one bit," he said sympathetically.

She watched the light play across the glass of the building and the trees around it a long moment. "I want to write about what happened," she told him in a rush of impulse. "From that last vid-phone call to this moment, I want to chronicle it all. Once I've done that, then I can come work with you. Deal?" She offered him her hand.

He took her hand in his, shaking it once. "Deal."

Three weeks later, Meris sat frowning at the tablet screen in front of her. Things weren't going as smoothly as she had expected. Not anymore. Parts were missing, and she didn't know what to do about it.

She tapped a fingernail on the arm of her chair. Darius. She needed to talk to him. And Wyll and Zac, too, most like. Decision made, she took the tablet and left her desk.

She took a slow breath and blew it out before knocking. A few seconds later, the wooden rounded-top door opened. The wounds on Darius' face had all healed, leaving one scar bisecting his right eyebrow – which matched the one on her own left brow – and one at the left corner of his upper lip. His broken fingers were still healing, but were now stabilized by thin, clear plastex sheath splints that were far less noticeable. He wore a gray shirt and lounge pants – and a surprised expression.

"Meris." His feet were bare. A hand towel was draped over his shoulder. Enticing scents wafted out from the kitchen at the other end of the house.

She held out the tablet. "The story is incomplete. It can't be just my perspective, my experience only. I need your help, your story. And Wyll's and Zac's. I need Myranda's, too, but I'll have to patch that together from her journal. I know she was keeping one on her tablet, I just need to get hold of it. Would Wyll have that or is it still at the Council Court in evidence?"

A slow smile crept into his eyes. "I'm not sure but we can find out easily enough. I'm making summer stew and almond bread; would you care to join me?" He held the door open wider and stepped aside. "You can fill me in on what you have written so far while I finish dinner."

"Thank you, that sounds nice." She realized her mistake then. "And hello," she added sheepishly.

A smile lit his face. "Hello."

She smiled back, crossing his threshold.

Don't miss out!

Visit the website below and you can sign up to receive emails whenever J.I. O'Neal publishes a new book. There's no charge and no obligation.

https://books2read.com/r/B-A-MNEF-RIKR

BOOKS 2 READ

Connecting independent readers to independent writers.

Did you love *Stell-Ore Justice*? Then you should read *The Crew of Cartage 15*[1] by J.I. O'Neal!

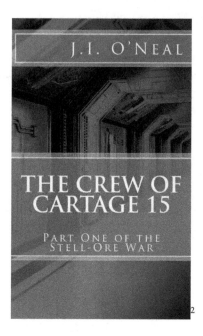

Would you risk starting a war to avenge the one you love?

When Meris Brand witnesses the brutal murders of her fiancé, Ellias, and his entire mining crew at the hands of Stell-Ore Mining Company's elite security unit, she storms the headquarters intent on taking down the only man who could have ordered the attack, Stell-Ore's Head of Operations, Darius Alazar.

Along the way, she enlists the help of the only Stell-Ore employee she can trust, Ellias' best friend, Berent Gaehts.

---

1. https://books2read.com/u/bwWG8G

2. https://books2read.com/u/bwWG8G

Soon, however, Meris learns that not everything is as it seems and there is far more to this story than she ever could have dreamed. And the one man who knows what really happened would sooner see Meris and her allies dead than reveal the truth - no matter the cost.

Received Honorable Mention in the L Ron Hubbard Writers of the Future Contest, September 2015.

Also by J.I. O'Neal

Riverdale PD Series
Impact: A Riverdale PD Series Prequel
Indiscriminate: 5th Anniversary Revised Edition
Time of Death

Stell-Ore War
The Crew of Cartage 15
Stell-Ore Justice